SALT BLOOD

KAORI KNIGHT

SALT BLOOD

Table of Contents

Acknowledgements

To the ones who bled onto the page with me,
Thank you.

To Jay, for giving this book its face. Your cover is the first spell readers see, and it's nothing short of magic.

To Blerd, for giving me the confidence I kept trying to bury. You reminded me that even shadows can stand in the light.

To my friends, who double-checked, reread, reassured, and never once complained about the chaos in my head, you held space for my doubt and still believed in the story anyway. You saw what I couldn't.

To every quiet moment where I nearly gave up: thank you for not lasting.

To the sea that kept my secrets,
The silence that sharpened my voice,
And the ghosts who wouldn't stop whispering,
This book is yours as much as mine.

And to the girl I used to be:
You survived.
You turned the wound into a spell.
You made it beautiful.

Prologue

The water near the castle is always cold. Colder than it should be. Dark. Darker than shadow, darker than grief. The kind of dark that remembers.

Nothing grows near the Citadel's edge. No flowers bloom, no birds sing. The fog eats color before the morning light can touch it. There is no warmth here. No real joy. Only ritual. Only decay.

Inside the palace, the halls echo with a silence too deliberate to be natural. The people outside wear mourning like a second skin. My parents, the Vampire King and the Swan Queen, speak in hushed tones, each word measured like poison in a chalice. They love me, I think. Or perhaps they once did.

But that was before.

Once, the kingdom thrived. I remember flickers of half-formed laughter, shadows dancing on sunlit cobblestones, songs rising from the sea. Then something broke. The joy didn't fade. It was ripped out, stolen by something older than monsters.

They blamed it on a curse. On a creature from the deep.

But I've lived long enough to know that monsters don't always come from the water. Sometimes, they wear crowns.

The beach is the only place that still feels like mine.

Here, the water is warm, inexplicably, as if it remembers me. As if it loves me. It's the only place I can breathe without thinking of what I am, what they made me. I come here when I can slip away, which isn't often.

I lay back in the sand, letting the hush of the tide lull me, until a voice sliced through the peace like a blade across silk.

"Aidina. Aidina. **AIDINA.**"

My eyes snapped open. My pulse stuttered.

Queen Visandra loomed on the cliff's edge, raven steed beneath her, gray-feathered robes trailing like smoke. Her presence turned the air sour.

I barely masked my sneer.

"Your Majesty," I muttered.

She didn't bother dismounting.

"Your father has been looking for you. This shore is forbidden unless accompanied."

"Of course it is," I said. "You've already ruined everything this place once meant to me. I suppose turning me into something cold and hollow is next on your list."

"Spare me," she said. "If it were up to me, this beach would be paved and salted. But your father, sentimental fool, spared it. For you."

"You've turned your back on the world."

"And yet," she said coolly, "it spins. Return. Now. That is your final warning."

She turned her steed, but I couldn't help it.

"The world you've come from will come for you, too. And not kindly."

She stopped. Shoulders still. Then she turned just enough for the wind to lift her hood.

Her eyes were crimson. Her teeth were too sharp to be human.

"Then let us be befallen, daughter."

She laughed as she rode away. Her guards remained behind, stone-faced. They didn't speak. But the water behind me did.

A ripple.

Then a roar.

Something moved beneath the surface, fast. Wrong.

The lead guard paled. Whatever it was, we wouldn't outrun it. Not with me here. He slammed his staff into a puddle, a ripple spread, a portal, trembling with cold light.

His gaze locked onto mine, a wordless apology.

And then he shoved me through.

I hit the stones hard.

The castle gates loomed in front of me. My father's expression shifted when he saw me, from relief to dread. My mother hissed orders before a servant handed her his sword. She offered it like a ritual, and he took it without a word. Regal. Terrible.

They stormed toward the war room. But I needed to see.

I ran to the window.

Outside, the courtyard had become a battleground. Not a siege, a hunt. The attackers came from the sea. Mercenaries, or something worse. Their eyes glowed like kelp-fire. Their blades left smoke in their wake.

And in the chaos, I saw her.

The shape of the tide. Towering. Ancient. Beautiful in the way death is beautiful.

Nessie.

The Loch Ness Monster. Real. And looking straight at me.

My heart surged. I turned to run, to find her.

And froze.

A man stood at the far end of the corridor. Pale skin. Hair white as ash. And his eyes, *a bright icy blue.*

Familiar.

My soul recognized him before my mind did.

"...Rahlin?" I whispered.

He stepped closer. His presence hollowed the air around him. I wanted to run to him, but something stopped me.

He unsheathed a short sword.

And lunged.

I barely dodged. The blade kissed my ribs.

My thoughts shattered. Why would he save me and then try to kill me? His name trembled on my tongue like something I'd carried through lifetimes.

He caught my throat. Pressed the blade to my heart.

I didn't resist. Not at first. Something inside me had gone quiet. Was it despair? Or was it recognition?

Then his grip faltered. He hesitated.

Something in him broke, just for a second.

He let me go.

I gasped.

And he kicked me, hard, through the window.

The wind shrieked as I fell.

I should've called on the water. I should've shifted, flown, vanished.

But I couldn't.

The shock, the pain, something inside me slipped.

Then, a figure caught me mid-fall.

Cold hands. Familiar. Desperate.

"Father," I breathed.

He held me as smoke rose from his back, the sun beginning to pierce the sky. His skin blistered. Blood streamed from his eyes.

"No, no, no, " I gasped, clutching him.

Then, a wind struck from above.

Feathers the color of dusk surrounded us. Visandra. Her robe became wings. Her face was pale with fury.

"Move!" she snapped. "I have you both."

She shielded him from the sun as he carried me into the foyer. The doors slammed shut behind us. Safe, for now.

We collapsed in a heap. I laughed, shaky, breathless, on the verge of sobbing. I clung to him. I didn't want to let go.

Visandra knelt beside me, arms extended. I took her hand. Hugged her.

She hesitated, then returned the embrace.

My father joined us. For one breath, we were whole.

"What happened?" he asked.

"There was a man... he saved me, then tried to kill me. I don't know where he went."

"What did he look like?"

"White hair. That's all I remember." I lied.

Because I couldn't tell them about the eyes. Not yet.

He pulled Visandra aside. She moved like a blade drawn from a sheath. Her wings rustled. Orders barked. Chaos danced behind the doors.

I turned back to the window.

Nessie was gone.

I wanted to ask about her, but the courtyard was full of fire and blood. There was no time, no room for questions, only dread.

My father returned, quieter now. He touched my face.

"Are you truly okay?" he asked.

I nodded, still watching the sea.

"Nessie is safe," he said lowly. "She returned to the water. I saw to it myself. We'll speak freely... later."

I smiled. Hollow.

Visandra stood in the doorway behind him; her silhouette stretched across the stones like a warning.

She hated Nessie. Always had. No one, not even my father, knows why.

I've tried to remember what happened the last time they met.

But every time I try, something blanks out.

Like a hole. Like rot.

But I'll find the truth.

Even if I have to bleed it out of the darkness myself.

When I finally came to, I was in my bedchambers, sweating. That was the worst dream yet.

Sometimes I truly cannot trust my own mind.

CHAPTER 1

The Phantom Citadel

Beneath a waning sky where stars blurred like lanterns drowned in fog, the Phantom Citadel stood sentinel on the edge of the marshlands, hidden just beyond the shore where silver waves kissed the beach. Its spires were woven from black coral and moonstone, rising like teeth from the mire; they were elegant, sharp, ancient, and waiting. Mist clung to its walls like breath to a grave.

To the uninvited, it was only legend. But within, it pulsed with life.

During the day, the Phantom Citadel shimmered like a dream carved from fog and coral. Nestled behind the beach, where the tide spoke in riddles, and the marsh breathed with secrets, it was built from sea-glass stone and bone-white towers. It rose from the brackish mire like a memory that refused to fade.

Its halls echoed with laughter.

Its foundations are with silence.

It was a place of beauty and blood, now at peace.

Laughter danced across the brine-salted air. Sirens flew overhead in whorls of ocean wind, their wings glistening with spray and light.

They darted in arcs through sea mist, singing to the sky in voices that could beguile the moon. Below, mermaids dove between lily-pool domes, their tails flicking silver trails through the water. Swan maidens danced barefoot on pale stones, casting shadows like falling feathers. The selkies lingered at the water's edge, quiet, protective, ever watching.

All clans lived together within the Citadel's bounds. Their peace was hard-won. Their council united.

And in the heart of it all stood Aidina, the daughter of two worlds, born from seafoam and shadow.

Her gaze swept the gathered citizens: gilled children chasing mothlight, salt-born merchants hawking charm-inked shells, selkies shifting between forms beneath the torches' glow. She could feel the harmony, taste it. And yet, a hollowness pulsed in her chest.

She was both sea and darkness, blood and brine.

Aidina moved like memory made flesh. A girl forged in grief, myth, and mystery. Her skin is a deep, warm caramel hue, marbled subtly with faint pearl undertones near her collarbones and cheeks, hints of her mermaid lineage surfacing like low tide. Her body is lithe, wiry with hidden strength, yet her presence feels heavier than her frame, a gravity born of bloodlines and buried truths.

Her hair is waist-length and ink-black with faint hints of crimson, coiling in the damp like seaweed with strands that shimmer red when the light strikes. Her eyes are stunning and disorienting. One is vivid emerald green, the other a fierce, unnatural red that pulses faintly when she's angry or afraid. However, they didn't always stay this way. On most days, they chose to stay either red or green. Her father always told her that they had a mind of their own. They're eyes that shouldn't belong in one face. They make you feel like you've forgotten something vital.

Aidina's limbs are elegant, her fingers often splayed like a swimmer's, as if the sea never quite lets go. Scars bloom like small constellations on her back, the remnants of spells, near-drownings, and failed resurrections. She wears practical armor with iridescent scales inset along her shoulders and spine, passed down from her mother's side.

But it's her voice, low, fragile, not always her own, that lingers. She speaks like someone chasing the echo of her own soul.

Though only nineteen, she was already a legend. A vampire mermaid, the first, last, and only of her kind. Some said she was cursed. Others said she was salvation. She only knew she was different and that something inside her had been missing for a long time.

Years of her memory. Gone. Stolen.

And no one would tell her why or how.

"Your Highness." The voice came from behind. It was calm, low, and warm like sealskin on a winter shore. Rahlin, her bodyguard and closest friend, bowed slightly. He was in his human form now: tall, broad-shouldered, pure white sea-wet hair clinging to his neck and sharp eyes like wet stone. His face is sharp yet kind. He had high cheekbones, a strong jaw, and a mouth more familiar with silence than speech. His eyes are ocean-gray with glints of green, like stormlight before a squall. He watches everything, but gives away nothing.

"You shouldn't wander alone," he said. "The tide is turning."

"It always turns," Aidina murmured, brushing her fingers through the black water. "But it never brings back what it takes."

Rahlin said nothing. He never did when the subject turned to her missing years. There was silence between them, not cold but cautious. It was as if some invisible current passed just beneath the surface, too dangerous to disturb.

She turned to Rahlin. "Does it ever feel too perfect?"

He tilted his head. "Everything perfect carries the seed of something broken."

"Is that selkie wisdom?"

"No," he smiled softly. "That's just me."

From the Citadel, the bell tolled.

It was time.

Aidina and Rahlin returned through the mist-veined halls where kelp vines clung to stone, and ghost light flickered in braziers made from sea-worn bone. All the clans had gathered: swan maidens in silver robes, sirens with folded wings, selkies in seal-leather armor, mermaids who could grow legs, coiled in spiral-shell jewelry, and the Citadel's citizens: humans touched by sea magic, born in fog and shaped by myth, their eyes always watching.

At the high table sat the Vampire King.

He was regal and terrible, his beauty carved in shadow. He was tall, lean, and dignified, yet haunted by his own history. His skin is a rich umber, smooth as polished stone, darkened by centuries beneath both sun and shadow. His cheekbones are high, his jaw elegant and sharp, and his eyes are deep-set, golden-red, and impossible to lie to, and they seemed to glow with internal fire. His hair, all black locks, also hints of red threaded in between. He and his daughter were twin flames in that regard. It's often tied back with an ornamental clasp carved from bone. His beard is finely trimmed and noble in shape but wild at the edges, like something that remembers what it once hunted.

His posture is regal but weary. His voice, a deep baritone, is laced with the softness of sorrow. Each word measured like the toll of a bell. He wears robes layered in velvet and leather, with a mantle of raven feathers and dried seaweed. He wore a pink pearl on his chest, a quiet tribute to his late wife, Queen Aleese. His crown is carved from driftwood soaked in blood.

He doesn't smile. He mourns, and rules, and bleeds in silence. Yet when he looks at Aidina, something warm tries to surface. Something deeply human.

He smiled at his daughter, but his gaze lingered too long. There was a secret there. One Aidina could feel in the marrow of her bones. And beside him, frozen like a statue of frost and vengeance, sat Queen Visandra.

Visandra is beauty weaponized. She walks like a goddess born in winter; she is aloof, brittle, and so elegant that it hurts to watch her move. Her skin is pale ivory, almost translucent near the temples. There is always something too still about her, as though her skin is stretched too tightly over bones that don't remember how to be human.

Her platinum-white hair is worn in elaborate braids woven with obsidian pins and blood-red ribbon. Her lips are a soft, unnatural pink, her teeth too perfect, and her eyes are an icy blue with no warmth. They watch the world like a distant predator. She is not cruel in expression, but every word she speaks carries the chill of long-dead water.

Visandra's swan wings emerge rarely, but when they do, they're vast and a beautiful snowy white. The feathers drip with shadow and illusion magic. Her voice is like a lullaby sung at your deathbed, too sweet to resist, too dangerous to trust.

She always wears white. Gowns with sleeves like wings and skirts like snowfall, stitched with silver thread and protective runes that no longer obey her.

Many whispered that she had not won the crown by love but by treachery. Her wings had been dipped in blood before they were cloaked in lace.

No one dared say it aloud. You could tell that this bothered Aidina. The rumors of Visandra's treachery overtook the memory of her mother in these halls.

Aidina barely remembered her mother. She had died when Aidina was eight, killed beneath suspicious silence. Or so she'd been told. But some nights, Aidina dreamed of her screams.

She was burning.

At the head of the chamber, the War Council assembled.

One leader from each clan: the Siren matriarch Madrelle, her eyes storm-dark and ancient. The Selkie Chief was cloaked in black fur. The eldest Mermaid, Queen Ylla, is blind but sees all. Thorne, a Citizen of the Phantom Citadel, robed in salt-stained linen and bearing the Mark of the Marsh. Even the Loch Ness Monster, wearing the face of a woman, tall, scarred, eyes too deep to be human, took her place beside them, shifting uneasily in her borrowed skin. Nessie's human form is strange and breathtaking, like a dream of a woman glimpsed in deep water. Her skin is a soft grayish-blue, like stone polished by tides. Her eyes are large and black as the deep with no whites, only pools of reflected memory and time. They seem to glow faintly in darkness.

Her hair is thick and dark and moves as though underwater, even in dry air. Woven through it are beads of fossilized coral and bone charms. When she smiles, her teeth are sharp and subtle, but until she laughs, they are not subtle at all.

Her limbs are long and slightly too flexible. Her fingers end in faint claws. Her gait is fluid, almost boneless, and when she walks, she rarely blinks. She wears sea-glass jewelry and layers of shawls or cloaks made from leviathan silk. Her voice is low, husky, and strangely touched by ages of shifting between forms.

She is ancient but feels young. Her humor is wry and dry, her emotions deep and unfathomable. To most, she's unsettling. To Aidina and her father, she's home.

The Siren Matriarch clicked her beak-like nails. "The Iron Islands are stirring again. Their trawlers have been seen in forbidden waters."

The Selkie Chief grunted. "If they come for the kelp fields again, we will not show restraint."

"The Coral Empire watches," rasped the old Mermaid Matron. "Their whispers reach us like poisoned waves."

Aidina listened. Every word etched a tremor into her spine. The outer nations were no longer dormant, and the peace was thinning.

And yet, the Queen, Visandra said nothing. Her eyes flicked toward Aidina like frost. When they met, it was like being cut.

Later, when the council ended, Aidina approached her.

"Why do you always look at me like a stranger?" she asked.

"Because you are," Visandra said, her voice cracking like ice underweight. "And you don't even know it."

Aidina's breath caught. "What does that mean?"

The Queen turned without answering, feathers brushing the marble-like falling snow.

Aidina's eyes narrowed as she watched her stepmother walk away. She was graceful, but hints of evil flickered in her eyes whenever she talked. Aidina should respect her, but every cold interaction chips away at that thin layer.

She felt a cold hand grasp her shoulder, and she already knew who it was. She looked back at her father, who smiled. He nodded, suggesting they take a walk.

Aidina and her father wandered the Citadel gardens, pools of still water bordered by whispering reeds. Here, hidden among the glowshrooms and star-anemones, she often came to remember what little she could of her mother, Queen Aleese.

From beneath the surface, she felt something stir, not from the pool, but from memory.

A flicker.

Her father, the Vampire King, felt the same. And decided to share a little bit of how he and her mother enjoyed each other's company every day for years on that beach Aidina enjoyed so much.

He spoke about his younger self, his hair wind-tangled, his scarlet eyes warm. He was standing waist-deep in water, drenched, laughing.

And Aleese, a vision of sunlit joy, spinning in the shallows, her tail gleaming of lavender and pearl. She twined her fingers through his as the tide lapped their waists.

"You'll wrinkle," he teased.

"I'm a mermaid, you brooding bat," she laughed, splashing him.

"I don't take back what I said," he laughed as he splashed her back.

"Then wrinkle with me."

It was a brief vision, but it left a warmth behind. Aidina smiled.

They continued walking until they came to the steps of the castle. As Aidina sat on the palace steps with her father, she asked, "Do you miss her?"

The Vampire King looked toward the horizon, where the moon bled silver over the sea. "Yes," he said softly. "Aleese was the ocean I drowned in. And I never wanted to surface."

He was no king for a moment, only a man who had once known joy.

Her father fixed her hair on his way into the castle, and Rahlin emerged from the shadows. He motioned for her to walk with him to the beach, and she was more than happy to oblige. Getting that particular memory from her father made her smile a little, but she still couldn't help but feel like there was something he was keeping from her.

Aidina walked barefoot along the shore, the waves tugging at her dress like curious hands. Rahlin joined her, his sealskin cloak draped over one shoulder, his still-damp hair tied loosely back.

"I hate secrets," she said.

"I know."

"I feel like everyone's watching me... but not for who I am. For what I was."

"You are Aidina," he said gently. "Daughter of the sea and the dark. That hasn't changed."

She looked at him. "Do you think the water remembers me?"

Rahlin knelt, trailing his fingers in the tide. "The water remembers everything. The only trick is learning to listen."

Aidina leaned her head on his shoulder. For a moment, the world felt simple again. After a while, he escorted her back to the castle, and she went to her room. His room was close to hers, of course, for her protection. But he didn't go into it often. He more or less stayed outside the castle on the beach.

Later in the night, restless, Aidina wandered the Citadel's old wing, a forgotten corridor where kelp grew through the cracks. She followed voices down the hall toward the observatory tower. Her father stood there with Nessie, the Loch guardian in human form. The air between them was thick with old grief.

"Is she starting to ask questions?" Nessie asked as she stared into the darkness of the castle.

"She remembers nothing," the Vampire King said. "And that's how it must remain."

"But if the truth ever resurfaces?"

"It will destroy her," he growled. "Just like it destroyed Aleese. And nearly destroyed me."

Aidina pressed her back to the wall, heart hammering.

"What did you do to me?" she whispered to the dark.

The wind howled from somewhere deep within the Citadel, and the ocean seemed to answer.

CHAPTER 2

Shadows Beneath Still Water

Aidina didn't sleep that night.

The words she overheard curled around her like smoke:

She remembers nothing.

That's how it must remain.

It will destroy her.

The idea of her father, one of the main souls she trusted implicitly, hiding something so grave from her was a weight she couldn't bear. Not alone.

The next morning, as the mist clung to the Citadel's walkways, she found Rahlin on the eastern beach, polishing the edge of his selkie blade. His sealskin rested across his shoulders, gleaming with salt.

She approached silently, but he looked up before she reached him. "Your steps are loud today."

"I need to talk to you."

His easy expression faded.

They walked along the shoreline until the Citadel's towers blurred behind the reeds. Aidina spoke, voice tight. "Last night, I heard my father and Nessie speaking. He said I don't remember something. Something that would destroy me if I knew."

Rahlin's brow furrowed. "What kind of something?"

"I don't know. That's the point."

He studied her face, clearly shaken. "Aidina... I have been with you almost every day since before the Vampire King truly assigned me to you. I don't remember anything terrible happening. If something had happened, I would've known. Wouldn't I?"

She looked away.

"Maybe someone made sure you wouldn't."

Rahlin was quiet momentarily, then said gently, "Ask him. Softly. When he's not being the King, just your father."

Aidina hugged her arms. "I'm afraid of what I'll find out."

"Then we'll find it together."

Aidina wanted to talk to her father, and she wanted to do it alone.

Rahlin offered to be there with her, but she needed to find out for herself. She went to the throne room, and her father sat atop his massive throne and massaged his temples. He was overthinking, as per usual. Between what was said at the War Council and the possibility of his daughter asking questions that he knew he shouldn't answer, he was feeling uneasy.

His eyes shifted, and he saw his daughter's coy smile as she stood before him. Before she could ask him anything, she felt the atmosphere get thick.

Visandra arrived the way winter does, without warning, and colder than expected.

Aidina stood beside her father in the throne room when the swan-maiden descended the long staircase, feathers trailing behind her like frost. The room stilled, and if anyone had been in there with them, they would have choked on the thickness of the tension. Her gown shimmered like ice over black velvet. Her eyes were sharp, bright, and colorless.

Her father fell in love with Queen Aleese, her mermaid mother, every day. Their laughter had filled the Citadel's high halls like sunlight on tidepools.

But this Queen... there was no sunlight here, only shadow.

Their wedding had been quiet, too quiet. The Vampire King's grief was still fresh. Visandra's presence was a sudden diplomatic alliance sealed not with joy but necessity.

And yet, now, she was Queen.

Aidina curtsied, her expression neutral. Visandra inclined her head just enough to acknowledge her. She didn't need to ask her stepdaughter to excuse herself as she was already out the door. Visandra and the Vampire King only had a quick conversation before she excused herself and left him to return to his racing mind. He hadn't even remembered that his daughter wanted to talk.

After a few minutes, Aidina passed too close to her stepmother in a corridor scented with salt and lilies.

"You smell of brine and blood," Visandra said without turning. "Just like your mother."

Aidina stopped. "Thank you."

"It wasn't a compliment."

"As if I don't know that," Adina replied, her voice. Calm. Dismissive.

As Visandra vanished around the corner, something cold settled in Aidina's chest.

There was hatred in the Queen's eyes.

And it had nothing to do with policy or power.

CHAPTER 3

The Silence Between the Waves

Far above the beach, deep into the night, two friends sat in a tower carved from moonstone and obsidian. The air shimmered with warding spells, protective, ancient, private.

The Vampire King poured sea-mint tea into two carved goblets. Across from him, Nessie sat in her human form, her long fingers tracing the edge of her cup.

"I think it's going to return to her," said the King quietly.

Nessie nodded. "You always knew it would."

"I thought the forgetting would be enough. That the pain would sink."

"Pain doesn't sink, old friend," Nessie murmured. "It waits."

The Vampire King stared down into the cup. "I see her walking the halls; she looks so much like Aleese. She comes into faint contact with me now, but when I look into her eyes... I see that night. And it guts me."

Nessie didn't answer at first. Then she said, "Aleese was one of the kindest queens I've ever known. She trusted too easily. But she loved deeply. She was fond of me, you know."

"I know. She said you were the first person in the Citadel who made her laugh after the crown settled on her head."

A silence stretched between them, not heavy, but sacred.

Then the Vampire King continued, voice hoarse: "She was the one who found the creature in the Citadel that night. She thought it was a siren, but its magic was twisted, corrupted. Something controlled it. It turned on her."

Nessie's gaze darkened. "And Aidina?"

"She heard the noise. She was sleepwalking, and she wandered into the hall. Aleese shielded her with her body. Took the strike."

He closed his eyes. "She used the last of her blood-magic to force a forgetting spell into Aidina's mind. She saved her... and then vanished into ash in my arms."

The cup shook in his hand.

"She made me swear to protect her. And to keep her from remembering. She said the darkness might return if the spell broke too soon."

Nessie looked at him sharply. "A good blood-magic memory spell can only be broken in two ways, neither of which have been done that I can sense. Do you think some other work was at hand?

"I don't know," the King whispered. "But the siren was never found. Only its feathered bones... and an echo."

"What kind of echo?"

The King met Nessie's eyes.

"A scream. Not of pain. Not of grief."

He paused.

"But of power."

Aidina couldn't sleep yet again. Her dreams turned into nightmares, and the nightmares refused to give her mind peace. So she wandered barefoot through the pale sands, the marsh wind teasing strands of her dark hair into her eyes. The sky was bruised with starlight, and the surf whispered against the shoreline like a voice trying not to be heard.

She found Rahlin where she always perched on his favorite driftwood log, half-shadowed by a tangle of beachgrass. His sealskin rested over his lap like a second soul. He didn't move when she approached.

"I thought you might come," he said softly, his eyes on the dark horizon.

"I couldn't sleep," she whispered.

He made space beside him. She sat, folding her legs and resting her shoulder lightly against his. They just listened to the waves for a time, two sea-bound creatures bound by something older than blood and gentler than silence.

Aidina spoke first. "Something's wrong with me."

"You're not broken, Aidina."

"I feel like I am. Like... there's a hole in me. And everyone is walking around it like it's not there."

Rahlin said nothing at first. Then: "Sometimes the worst wounds don't leave blood."

She turned toward him. "All this time with me and you don't remember anything strange?

His brow furrowed. "No. I would have told you. I would've remembered. You know I would."

"But that's just it." Her voice cracked. "Is it not so clear that someone made sure you wouldn't?"

That silence between them became deeper and more charged. Rahlin turned fully toward her. His fingers brushed her hand. "If something happened... if something was done to you, I swear, I'll help you find the truth. Even if it was taken from both of us."

Her fingers tightened on his. "What if I shouldn't know?"

"You're strong enough to carry it."

"I'm not."

"You are."

Aidina exhaled shakily. "Sometimes, I dream of blood in the halls. And my mother's voice singing. But when I wake up, I can't remember the tune."

Rahlin pulled her into his arms then. Slowly, gently, like he'd been waiting to do it for years.

Her head rested against his shoulder, and his sealskin was cool beneath her fingertips. She breathed him insalt, kelp, and the scent of deep water. His heartbeat was steady and grounding.

He stroked her hair with careful fingers. "You know what the water taught me?" he murmured.

"What?"

"It holds everything, storms and calm, rage and peace. It never stops. It never forgets. But it forgives."

Aidina closed her eyes. "I don't know if I can forgive someone for taking my memory."

"Maybe you don't have to yet," he said. "Maybe just start by forgiving yourself for not remembering."

She smiled, barely, but it was real. "When did you get so wise?"

"I grew up chasing a girl who thought jellyfish were secret messengers," he teased. "She made me listen harder."

"Sounds like she was pretty magical."

Rahlin's voice softened to something just shy of a confession.

"She still is."

As the tide pulled moonlight across the sand, Aidina stayed curled beside Rahlin. The gentle quiet between them stirred old memories, and after a long pause, she asked, "Do you remember the first time we met?"

Rahlin laughed softly. "You mean the time you tried to drown me?"

"I *pulled* you into the sea," she corrected with a smirk. "It's not my fault you panicked."

"I was thirteen and wearing full armor," he said dryly. "And I was told *not* to touch the crown princess."

"You did anyway."

"You dared me."

They both chuckled, and the tension began to ease like fog pulling away from the surface of deep water.

After her laughter faded, Rahlin added quietly, "That was the day I asked to be assigned to you in a more official and personal capacity."

"You were just a squire."

He nodded. "But you told me the water spoke to you. That it hummed when danger was near."

"I remember," Aidina said softly.

"The Court didn't believe you. But I did." He looked out at the sea. "That night, when the tide pulled too far, and the Citadel flooded in the northern hall... you were the only one who saw it coming. You saved twenty people. Including me."

"And after that?"

"I went to your father and said I'd serve you until death. He laughed. Thought it was noble. And told me that I've had that job since we were small."

Aidina tilted her head. "He made you fight a shadowbeast in the coliseum."

Rahlin winced. "Two, actually."

"You didn't even flinch."

"I was already yours, and I'd do anything."

Rahlin went quiet, then said, "But the real trust came later, didn't it? That night in the Bone Marsh."

Aidina felt her chest tighten. "I thought you were going to die."

"You carried me across the swamp on your back," Rahlin said, still slightly amazed. "Bled half your soul into me to keep me from slipping into the Deep."

"I didn't think. I just... couldn't lose you."

He looked down at her now, his expression open and steady. "You won't."

Her throat tightened. She knew that she was safe in his arms. But he knew, just like she did, she would never be happy until she found what she had lost. It was the hole that only continued to get bigger the longer she was without answers.

It was quiet there on the beach. Unknown to them and the rest of the Citadel on land, the sea stirred. It was truly disturbed.

Far below the Citadel, where the kelp forests bent like cathedrals and ancient pressure pressed against the ocean floor, two shadows met in the dark.

The Siren Leader, Madrelle, her wings slick and translucent like spun glass, hovered in the ruins of a forgotten shrine. Across from her floated Queen Ylla, her ink-black scales, silver hair braided with coral, and her blind eyes like shattered opal.

Between them pulsed a sphere of binding magic.

A siren floated motionless within it, her eyes pitch-black, lips slightly parted. Veins glowed with red and violet light. Her feathers were ragged, her talons twitching with echoes of a forgotten command.

"She hasn't spoken since the night of the attack 11 years ago," Ylla said. "Her mind is... scrambled. But her magic is still tuned to the one who controlled her."

Madrelle's wings flicked nervously. "She didn't act alone."

"No," Ylla agreed. "But she's the only link we have to what happened to Queen Aleese."

"And the girl?" Madrelle asked.

"She remembers nothing. For now."

The siren within the sphere blinked just once.

Both leaders swam back.

"She stirs," Ylla whispered. She may not have been able to see this creature, but she could feel the evil lurking inside of her. They both knew this could lead to more danger than it was worth. But they were too fond of the King and his daughter and would do anything to ensure the truth would be uncovered. Darkness lurked in their waters, and they would not stand for it.

After she visited with Rahlin, Aidina crept through the moonlit upper corridor. She was on her way to bed, but she couldn't help but overhear the echo of voices that were raised too loud to ignore. Her father's chambers were just ahead. It was usually at this time that Rahlin would encourage her off to bed, but he chose to stay down on the beach.

As she approached the corner wall adjacent to her father's room, she heard that grating voice again.

"I did not agree to a marriage just to become a figurehead," Visandra's voice hissed.

"You are not a figurehead," the Vampire King growled. "You are queen, but your place was taken with power, not affection."

Aidina froze in the shadows, barely breathing.

"Oh?" Visandra laughed bitterly. "And what would your precious Aleese say of this arrangement? Or are you still pretending you've buried her, even though you keep her dagger under your bed?"

A long silence.

Then, her father's voice was low and cutting. "Careful."

"You think your secrets keep you in control. But I *know your true name,* husband. The one that got locked away before you took the throne."

Aidina's heart stopped.

A name? His real name?

"How? You wouldn't dare speak it."

"I don't need to," Visandra said. "I just need you to know that I could."

A sudden gust of wind muffled the following words, the hallway trembling with ambient magic.

Aidina backed away slowly, her heartbeat wild.

His name.

The siren.

The forgetting spell.

Everything was beginning to circle her like sharks.

And the water was rising.

CHAPTER 4

The Weight of a Name

I thought I knew my father.

He ruled the Phantom Citadel with silence and shadows, a monarch of marble eyes and quiet dread. But I realize something terrible as I pore over the brittle tomes in the sunless archive, ink swimming in blood-red candlelight.

I do not know his name.

Not his real one. Not the one whispered to him when he was still small enough to need cradling before the thrones were cold and the courtyards overgrown with thorns. The records speak only of "the King" or "the Shadow Prince." They fear specificity. Even the pages recoil from the truth.

I touch my own throat and whisper: *What was your name?*

And the silence of the Citadel whispers back: *You forgot.*

But how can I forget that which I've never heard?

How could he forget something as powerful as his name?

In the damp, shadowy corners of the Phantom Citadel, where whispers roamed like hungry phantoms, I sought a truth buried deeper than the catacombs beneath our marshy loch. A flickering candle barely illuminated the brittle pages of the ancient tome I clutched, the leather covers worn and cracked with age as if they bore the wounds of forgotten memories. I leaned closer, heart racing with anticipation and dread, the words spilling secrets I was desperate to uncover.

Who was my father?

It seemed like such a simple question, yet my mind was uncertain.

Every time I thought I brushed against the edges of his identity, a cloud of fog consumed it.

How do I not know his name? Did *anyone* know it?

My heart sank, the chill of the damp air creeping down my spine, wrapping around me like the heavy coils of an invisible serpent. I was a girl caught between the breaking waves of a sea I could no longer remember and the sticky shadows of a past that eluded me.

My father, the Vampire King of the Phantom Citadel, occupies a throne carved of darkness and despair. He is a striking figure, with eyes that gleam like polished obsidian, highlights of that blood red that chills your spine, and a presence that commands the air we breathe. My father doesn't speak of his past, so all I have are tales of his reign, echoes of a mysterious past that made my heart ache for memory and the connection I yearn to reforge.

As I turned the fragile pages, the air grew thicker, charged with energy as if the very walls of the Citadel clamored for their voices. Each book spoke of my father in the highest regard. But it only continued to feel like something was missing. The story unraveled before me, revealing a heart-wrenching truth that seeped into the cracks of my soul. There is one book that resists decay. Bound in something that smells faintly of seawater and rust, it opens with a moan and bleeds memory. I read it slowly and carefully. It is not written, it is remembered, not in ink, but in emotion.

And this is what it tells me:

He was not born of the Citadel. He came to it bloodstained and barefoot; a foundling dragged from some midnight massacre beyond the Black Pines. The Queen, Rani, childless for a night more, pressed her lips to his forehead and called him *blessing*. The King, Cynric, whispered *heir*, and the castle thrummed with something like hope.

Years passed, and sons were born of the Queen's blood, three of them: radiant, firm, and warm, with the sun still in their smiles. The three of them got along with their older brother. They either didn't realize or didn't care that he wasn't of their blood. They lived in peace and became their own individual selves. I couldn't help but frown.

He never speaks of siblings.

I turned the page to reveal their names: Siran, Lyeth, and Corvan. They had been raised with him in happiness.

I found an entry tucked into a side margin: " *One sought peace. One sought power. One fell in love with the sea.* "

It sounded as if they were four sides of the same person. They laughed together, they played together, and they even trained together. There was not one time when they were truly separate until they had gotten older and settled into their mindsets. And even then, the plan was always to be together.

And yet, one by one, they withered.

Not swiftly. Not gruesomely. Quietly, as if fading into mist. The healers found nothing. The Queen wept herself raw. But the King... he watched the adopted boy with growing certainty. He noticed over everything happening that the Citadel had welcomed him, an orphaned vampire cradled in the arms of a King and Queen who adored him as their own. And even though my father was not a natural-born prince, and their true sons began to perish, one by one, the Citizens looked to my father with hope and faith. At the same time, Queen Rani started to look at him with distrust and hate.

It was a tale dripped in horror, wrapped in the tendrils of mystic power and betrayal. I shuddered as I read the final moments of the King's life, laid bare in desperate confession. So there on his deathbed, flesh withered like old paper, the King spoke to his adopted son alone.

"I have sinned," he croaked.

My father held Cynric's hand. His grip loosened as he braced for the news. But it was never what he imagined. He almost thought his father would tell him that he had always hated him, as the Queen had. But this was not the news that hit his ears.

"I fed them poison in their wine, one by one. I had to, don't you see? You were the future. The others... they burned too bright."

The boy, no longer a boy, stood silent as if the crown on his brow weighed more than the world.

"They were your sons," he whispered.

"They were never enough," said the King.

It was he who had killed his sons.

The old King, King Cynric, spoke with trembling lips, his heart heavy under his guilt and the weight of his actions suffocating as he revealed that the throne belonged not to blood but to the chosen. The King died with a smile, and my father let his hand fall to the side of the bed, standing in genuine disbelief. All this time, he secretly blamed himself for the death of his brothers. He thought he had become a monster in the middle of the night. But it was never that, no. It was their own father. *His* own father.

The Queen felt the loss as a fracture in her soul. But when she found the truth, and she did, her grief became rage. But she wasn't just mad at her husband, but at her son as well. Her grief and rage blinded her. She made herself believe my father was in on the plan. My father was a victim.

Rage-induced, she called the old gods beneath the Citadel, the ones the stones remember.

"I cannot kill him," she said. "But I will unmake him."

And with a curse older than death, she tore his name from every tongue, every book, every heart.

"You shall reign nameless," she hissed. "You shall forget your shape, your self, your seed. You will become a shadow, and the Citadel will mourn without knowing why."

She died as the last syllable of the curse turned her to salt. And just like that, my father's fate unfurled, a curse laid upon him by a mother who had loved but was betrayed by her husband's madness. The Queen, spectral with grief, had turned her sorrow into vengeance, casting a spell so vile that it stole away his name, the very essence of who he was, the only thing left of his blood family. The Citadel, too, was bound by her magic, forgotten remnants of history cascading into shadows, a prison woven of despair. The weight of his lost name pressed against my heart, echoing the sorrow of generations.

The air thickened with emotion, and as I pieced the fragments together, I could almost hear my father's anguished whispers, an echo of confusion and longing that pricked at the edges of my mind. I was his daughter, yet I felt as nameless as he in the lore of this place. Was there a way to break the spell, reach beyond the misty veil of memory, and reclaim identities lost in time's cruel grip?

But with every revelation came a deepening dread of what I might uncover. Would I find my father's name at the cost of my own, or would the history I unearthed lead to my demise? The shadows danced ominously around me as if the secrets of the Citadel were a living, breathing entity, waiting, watching, and watching.

I closed the book. The candle had nearly died, and so had my breath.

The Citadel hums softly around me, its stones weeping memories I can't hold.

He never told me this because he does not remember, and I am the only one who can return his name.

But if I do... will the curse break?

Or will I?

At that moment, I made a silent promise to unearth the truth, to confront whatever specters of the past I had inherited. Because, as haunting as it was, I needed to know not just my father's name but the fate that awaited the girl, a vampire, a mermaid, a prisoner of an unbroken spell, tangled in love, loss, and the shadows of a citadel that never forgot.

I've had enough of the secrets and lies. I wanted the truth, for once. I went to my father. Rhalin was already in the room with him, awaiting orders like he did every morning. I didn't even realize I had spent so long down there.

I slammed the book on the marble table in my father's private solar.

My father looked up slowly, his red eyes unreadable.

"Why didn't you tell me?" I asked, my eyes meeting his. "About your siblings. About your name."

Rahlin stood quietly nearby, tense.

The King exhaled. "Because grief like that can crack the world open."

"You always said names had power."

"They do," he said softly. "Mine nearly destroyed me."

I was trembling when I approached him. "You locked it away after they were murdered."

The King's hands clenched. "They weren't murdered. They were *sacrificed*. By the man who called himself my father. And I didn't lock it away; it was *stripped* from me."

Rahlin stepped forward. "Why?"

"Because they made choices," he said. "Siran turned his back on the crown, became a scholar, and wanted to bargain for peace. Corvan... fell in love with a selkie and planned to abdicate. And Lyeth tried to overthrow the King and stop the blood feasts. A different form of peace. Peace by force."

My father looked at me, his heart shattered. "I survived. Barely. And I promised myself that no one would ever control me again."

"Even if it meant forgetting who you were?" I whispered.

"Yes."

"You let her take it. You knew the truth. She knew the truth. And you *knew* that she knew the truth. You didn't even bother to try to talk her out of it? To defend yourself? Your name?"

"My name was nothing but pain, not only for her but for me. Every day, I heard it, not theirs, and it killed my soul. I knew that the throne was not mine. And I took it anyway."

"He...he gave it to you."

"He did. And it cost me my *brothers*. It cost me my *parents*. And it cost me *my name*. I should have done more. I should have fought for them. And I didn't. And because I didn't, I don't deserve the name."

The room quieted.

I lowered myself into the nearest chair. "Tell me the rest. Tell me about my mother. Did *she* know your name?"

The King looked at Rahlin. Rahlin gave a single nod.

He spoke slowly, like turning a blade in old wounds. "I don't know if she knew. The spell applied to the entire kingdom at the time. She only ever called me loving names. Names of endearment.

She was the one I loved more than my name, and then along came you. Someone else I loved more than that damn name. And then came that night. Aleese died saving you. The creature that attacked her... was a siren. Enchanted, controlled, perhaps even possessed. But deadly. It tore into our home with no warning."

I shook my head. "But I saw nothing? I,"

"You only don't remember not seeing anything," Rahlin said gently, trying to ease the vague explanation. "It sounds like she used her final breath to protect you. And to take the memory."

The King reached out and touched my cheek lovingly and cautiously.

"She erased it because she didn't want you to carry it. But it cost her everything."

He looked at Rahlin, who seemed just as confused because this part of his memory was also gone.

"You were in the castle that night as well. You were found near them a little way down the hall. The blood was all over the floor. The spell was still lingering and working, and we believe that when you touched Aidina, it also worked on you. You may have stumbled to get help. But no one else was there that night, so it is hard to be sure."

"And now?" I whispered.

"Now... that spell is breaking."

CHAPTER 5

The Council in Shadow

The moment he said it, the air shifted. A sudden hush fell over the Citadel.

The windows were clouded with mist. Somewhere in the distance, water crashed against stone. The floor beneath their feet *shivered*, not from movement, but from memory.

Aidina clutched her chest. Something was *unfolding* inside her. A flicker of screams. A flash of silver hair. Blood in the water.

"She's starting to remember," Rahlin said.

The King stood. "Then we have no time."

The Shadow Hall had not been summoned in years.

Now, it bloomed open beneath the Phantom Citadel like the throat of some ancient, slumbering beast. Carved from black coral and sunken stone, its vaulted ceiling seemed to swallow light, and the dark water covered the table like a sheet. The war banners of each people, swan maiden, selkie, vampire, mermaid, siren, and the druidic citizens of the marsh hung still and heavy in the dark.

Aidina stood beside her father at the obsidian table. Her eyes flicked over the gathered leaders, her skin prickling with unease.

To her left, Queen Ylla of the Merfolk floated slightly above her seat, her hair like moonlit riverweed. Across from her, Madrelle of the Skyborn Sirens folded her wings tight, shadows pooling at her feet. The Selkie Warden, gray-bearded and robed in sealskin, stood beside Rahlin, who represented Aidina's voice when she was too overwhelmed to speak.

Next to Madrelle stood High Warden Thorne, a quiet man with moss on his shoulders, one of the Citizens, old as the Citadel itself, who rarely left the marshes. Visandra was absent, but she was never part of this. So it wasn't noted.

Aidina caught her father's glance. He gave her a slight nod. She straightened.

The Vampire King's stern stare at the leaders told them everything they needed to know. Aidina was remembering. Subtlety was no longer required.

Queen Ylla spoke first.

"There has been... movement. At the deepest trench, where the Siren Prison is kept."

The chamber stilled.

"We strengthened the wards," Madrelle said, her voice sharp. "No one has entered. Nothing has escaped."

"No one *living,* perhaps," murmured the Selkie Warden.

"What do you mean?" the Vampire King asked.

Ylla raised a hand and conjured a flickering illusion over the table, a pulsing ripple of deep and slow red blooming like blood in the water.

"This magic appeared near the prison two nights ago. It is the same frequency as the one that controlled the siren who... attacked Queen Aleese over a decade ago. "

Aidina felt her stomach twist.

"*You* have had her this entire time?" The Vampire King stiffened.

"We captured her that night. She tried to kill several mermaids and sirens; she needed to be stopped," Madrelle responded, as if the King should have known that.

"And there's more," Ylla continued. "The magic that has kept her in this catatonic state is not only awakening. It's *calling.*"

The illusion shifted, a spiral now, faint but unmistakable.

"A summoning circle," Rahlin breathed.

"Someone is trying to free the siren," the Citizen Warden murmured. "Or awaken what remains of her mind."

"Why not destroy her?" Thorne asked.

Madrelle's wings rustled. "Because something rides her thoughts, and it is not born of our world."

The Vampire King leaned forward, red eyes burning. "Are you saying there's an *outsider* in the Citadel?"

"We're saying," said Ylla, "that the past is not dead. Only drowning."

As the Council erupted into strategies and territorial blame, Aidina's thoughts blurred. *The same magic. The same siren.* Her mother's blood. Her stolen memory.

She stood suddenly, interrupting the chaos.

"If someone's trying to reach her," she said, her voice shaking, "they already know she's there. Which means someone has betrayed us. Who else knew she was there?"

All eyes turned to her.

Madrelle's wings flared. "Careful, Princess. Not every shadow is treason."

"And not every silence is loyalty," she snapped back.

Her father placed a hand gently on her shoulder. "Enough."

Aidina sat slowly. But her mind didn't quiet.

Thorne, surprisingly enough, nodded in agreement with the princess.

"She's not wrong. Betrayal is not uncommon here."

Queen Ylla stood, magic sparking in her fingertips. " We need answers, now. I also agree that the princess is not incorrect. We may not have been in the castle that night, but something is definitely off."

Rahlin's hand brushed Aidina's gently under the table. Her father's eyes, hollow and burning, never left her face.

The spiral in the illusion turned blood-red.

And deep in her bones, Aidina remembered the scream she had never let herself hear.

The Shadow Hall thickened with tension.

A noticeable space lay where Queen Visandra's seat should be, draped in pale feathers and rose gold, now vacant and gathering dust.

"She should be invited to these things," muttered the Selkie Warden.

"For what? Unless she has extra knowledge to present or advice to give, we don't need her," Queen Ylla said, her mouth tight.

"Maybe we need to keep eyes on her," added Madrelle. Her wings twitched.

Aidina shifted in her chair. *Why would they need to watch Visandra now? Unless she already knows something, or maybe they too don't trust her...*

High Warden Thorne leaned forward, his voice like shifting mud. "We must address the deeper truth: no siren should be capable of what this one did. Mindless violence, perhaps. But enchantment? Possession? That is not siren magic."

Madrelle hissed. "It is not *natural* siren magic. And we are more than *just* mindless violence, High Warden. Please be sure to remember that."

Ylla summoned the illusion again, the siren's psychic pulse twisting across the table in spirals of black and red. "This is not of our world. It is *ancient*. Older than this Citadel. Older than the marshes. A song warped and inverted."

"Which means," Rahlin said slowly, "someone *bound* her."

"And who," growled the Vampire King, "has that kind of power?"

No one answered.

Then Nessie stood.

She had been quiet the entire meeting, her long limbs folded like branches, her water-moss hair pinned with silver stones. Her voice was deep, steady, and soft as a lake before a storm.

"Perhaps I should go down to her."

Heads turned.

The Vampire King raised an eyebrow. "You think you can undo her?"

"I can hear her. I will not pretend I can fully heal her," Nessie replied. "But I can break what's bent. If her soul is twisted, I will help straighten it. If there's something buried in her mind, I can find it. I've brought others back before."

"You can restore memories?" Aidina asked, breath catching.

"I can do more than that, child," Nessie said, knowing precisely what Aidina was asking. "If your mother's soul left a mark, I can find it. If the enchantment clings to your bones, I can unmake it. But I must be close. And you must be brave."

Aidina nodded silently.

"And," Nessie added, "I believe the siren will speak to you. You were present when she killed your mother. That ties you."

"She doesn't even know me," Aidina said.

"Oh," Nessie said with a half-smile, "I believe she knows exactly who you are."

The Council murmured, shifting toward consensus.

Queen Ylla asked the final question: "What will you ask her?"

Aidina stood. Her voice rang clear.

"I will ask her who sent her, why she came, and what she remembers."

"Be prepared," said Thorne. "She may not be the only one who remembers."

When everyone left the chambers, the King pulled Nessie to the side,

"Is there something I'm missing here, *old friend*?"

Nessie simply smiled and patted his shoulder.

"*We* will speak another time, my friend."

CHAPTER 6

The Chamber Below, The Truth Above

The Abyssal Chamber, the underwater prison that held the most dangerous threats to the Citadel, felt like the eye of a drowned god.

Aidina followed Nessie through a spiral of submerged tunnels, salt-bricked, rune-etched, and cold with the ancient breath of the sea. Lanterns flickered with violet fire, their reflections bending across the waterlogged walls. Every sound echoed, even her heartbeat.

The siren hung motionless in a column of thick, shimmering brine, bound by cords of sea-sung magic. Her body looked half-stone, half-moonlight, neither asleep nor fully awake.

Nessie's voice was almost tender. "Stay close. If she stirs, speak truth. But do not promise anything."

Aidina gave a slight nod. "She's truly been like this for all this time?"

"She has. Which is not only uncommon but also dangerous; however, something awoke her last night, and we need to figure out what."

Nessie placed a palm against the brine column. The glass rippled. A soft, low, mournful hum followed, the same melody Nessie sang when calling storms.

The siren opened her eyes.

No irises. No pupils. Just bottomless, swirling ink.

Aidina stepped forward, voice trembling. "You... knew my mother."

The siren smiled without parting her lips. It was not a kind smile.

"I knew her light," she whispered. "I swallowed it."

Aidina flinched.

Nessie's voice stayed calm. "Why did you attack Queen Aleese?"

The siren's body rippled slightly, as though disturbed by an unseen current.

"*She* was in my way. I was *sent*. My will was drowned. I was only a mirror for a voice that was not mine."

"Who sent you?" Aidina asked.

The siren's head tilted.

"The one who *needed* the Queen gone. The one who needed the child *devoured*. The one who learned how to twist the sea into a blade."

Nessie's breath caught. "Twist the sea..."

The siren continued, eyes locked on Aidina. "You were meant to die. But it didn't happen. At least not *then*. The voice was angry when Aleese intervened. You were spared. Spared wrongfully in fact."

Aidina stepped closer. "Then? Explain. What happened to me?"

Nessie tilted her head to the ground, preparing for the answer she knew would be revealed.

The siren's neck turned sharply, unnaturally. "You *died*. Just not that night. But later. By a *trusted hand*."

Aidina went cold.

Nessie whispered, "What are you saying?"

The siren swayed in her prison. "You walked into the dark three years ago and barely came back. But something else wore your skin until your true power invaded it again. With your soul restored, she had more to hate. She is waiting to finish it."

"She?" Aidina asked. "Who is she?"

The siren laughed, and cracks formed in the water around her.

"You *know* her. She watches you still. She wears white. She smiles. And she *never forgets* what she lost when Aleese still had breath."

Aidina's hands began to tremble. "Who else was there that night?"

The siren's eyes flared.

"Two shadows. There was the one who *wept*. And then she ordered me to finish what she could not begin. And then there was the one who simply looked on, accepting the failure that had become."

Aidina shook her head in confusion. "You're saying the *witness*... the one who *wept* was also the one who *sent* you?"

The siren's voice fell to a whisper:

"A queen with feathers does not fly without blood on her wings."

With that, her body twisted sharply in the brine. She screamed, and the magic holding her in prison began to *groan*. Runes on the glass flared red-hot.

Nessie grabbed Aidina's arm. "We have to go. Now."

Aidina didn't move. Her fingers pressed against the brine.

"What else did I forget?" she pleaded.

The siren's final whisper curled around her like seaweed:

"You forgot how to scream."

The waves whispered as they always had, but now they sounded different.

Aidina sat at the edge of the tide pool below the Phantom Citadel, where the water shimmered with soft pink moss and fireflies. Her knees were drawn to her chest, her wet hair clinging to her shoulders. She couldn't look at the water without seeing *her*.

Her mother's face was burning away in a flicker of moonlight. The siren's voice still clung to her bones like brine:

"You forgot how to scream."

Nessie stood a few feet away, silent, giving her space.

Aidina broke the silence. "Do you think she could have done it?"

Nessie did not pretend to misunderstand.

"I think Visandra is capable of many things," she said softly. "But I also think she's very good at making *others* do them for her."

"She was there that night," Aidina whispered. "The siren all but said it. She watched. She knew I was supposed to die. But she isn't the one who *wept*."

Nessie's face was unreadable. "And yet she married your father so long afterward."

Aidina's fingers dug into the sand. "She knew my mother's magic saved me. So, she killed me later? Why don't I know my own mind?"

"Because you weren't supposed to remember. And perhaps some feared what else you'd remember if that spell broke."

Aidina looked up sharply. "You said you could restore memories."

"I can," Nessie said. "But magic that buries trauma does so for a reason. Sometimes memories are lost to protect the soul."

"I want to remember," Aidina said, voice cracking. "Even if it kills me...again." That last word felt like rotten sand on her tongue.

Nessie's gaze softened. "Then I will help you. But know this: the moment you remember, *you will never be the same*."

Aidina didn't blink.

"Good," she said. "Because I'm already not."

Far above the tide pools, in a hall that smelled of dust and bone, Rahlin stood before Queen Visandra.

The room was quiet. Her pale eyes gleamed beneath a veil of feathers. She stood at the center of an ancient spiral of painted runes. They were older than the Citadel itself.

"You've served her well," Visandra said, circling him slowly. "Loyal. Steadfast. Unquestioning."

Rahlin said nothing.

She stepped closer. Her fingers brushed his cheek.

"But you don't remember the day it happened, do you?" she murmured. "You were *there*, sweet seal-boy. And then you weren't. Just like *her*."

"I don't understand," Rahlin said, voice tight.

"No," Visandra said, touching his forehead with a single, ice-cold finger, "but you will."

Her nail pressed into the space between his eyes.

The moment contact sparked, Rahlin screamed a raw, shattering sound as his body arched backward. His eyes lit like blue fire, veins glowing beneath his skin as if filled with starlight and sea salt.

The runes around them pulsed. A heartbeat of *forgotten power* passed through the air.

Visandra whispered:

"Let it in. Let what was locked be loosed again."

Pain wasn't the right word. Pain had shape, rhythm, reason. This was something else.

As Visandra's nail pressed to his brow, Rahlin's body convulsed. Magic, not his own, ripped through him. A blue flame burned behind his eyes, and in its light, something ancient unlocked.

A memory not his, but *buried* in him.

He saw fractured pictures, which hit him quickly: a cold and damp stone hallway echoed with footsteps and distant laughter.

Soon after, Aidina, just eight, barefoot and confused, holding a candle. She looked over her shoulder and whispered, "Mama?"

A creature of wings and salt, black-eyed and thrashing, charging down the corridor.

Queen Aleese, emerging from her chambers with wind and ocean at her back. She screamed Aidina's name.

The Queen raised her hands. Light and sea foam bloomed, and she channeled every drop of her life into a barrier.

Rahlin, so young at the time, clutched his trident and was ready to protect the one he loved. He rushed into the corridor... but froze as Visandra stepped out of the shadows in front of him and placed two fingers to his temple.

"Sleep," she whispered.

And the world went black.

Rahlin snapped back to the present, gasping, as if drowning.

He was on his knees, trembling. Visandra stood over him, composed and serene.

"You saw it," she whispered. "Good. Now be quiet."

Her hand hovered above his chest. "You won't speak of it until I will it."

But something burned in Rahlin's chest. A thread of defiance, sewn with Aidina's laughter, her stubbornness, how she once offered him a shell and said, *"You're mine now, you know. My knight of sea and sky."*

His lips parted. "You killed her."

Visandra smiled.

"Not by my own hand. I merely watched."

He was so suddenly out of breath and out of words. But his eyes flickered with the past and pain.

Aidina paced the royal garden, what remained of it. The vines had grown wild, and the roses bloomed in blood-red spirals, untamed.

Nessie waited beside her, leaning against the fountain where Aleese used to sing.

"Are you sure?" Nessie asked.

Aidina nodded. "I need answers. No more riddles. I'm done being protected."

She stormed into the Citadel. Past the thrones. Past the tapestries of vampire conquests and sea-queen peace treaties. Past the rusted doors of the cathedral, where they used to pray to the Old Blood Moon.

She found her father alone in his study, staring at a shattered mirror.

His long black hair fell around his shoulders. His eyes, scarlet as a setting sun, met hers.

"You found the book," he said quietly. "About my name. I hid it so deep because it wounded me. Is that all you found?"

Aidina didn't answer. She stepped closer.

"Why didn't you tell me I *died?*"

The room stilled.

He closed his eyes. "Because I couldn't bear to lose you again."

Nessie entered, closing the door behind her.

"You need to tell her," she said gently.

"Did Visandra kill me?" Aidina asked

The Vampire King sank into his chair.

"No. She was with me when we got the report that you were missing. We had just returned from Silya to celebrate your birthday, but I was too late," he whispered. "Your mother died in my arms at the start of the new moon when you were eight. Around your sixteenth birthday, I went looking for you after we learned you hadn't been seen, and I found you on the beach in a pool of your blood in Rahlin's arms. I didn't know what to do. It was like looking in a mirror all those years ago, and Visandra said that even the darkest of dark magic couldn't save you."

Aidina's hands trembled. "But I'm here."

"Yes," he said, voice barely audible.

"Because I had someone I trusted more than life itself, who used the last of their blood to bring you back. We didn't know if it would work, but I was desperate to try. It wasn't until later that we realized the spell your mother did as she gave her life for you on a completely separate night would not only take your memories of that night, but it would completely wipe out the memory of your death as well. A last spell of protection, provided by my one true love. A spell to keep you sane for as long as possible. And Visandra has always hated you for that."

A silence like a funeral bell followed.

Aidina looked at him through tears. "Then why marry her?"

His mouth twisted. "Because I thought I'd lost everything. And she promised to help me rebuild."

"Do you think she killed my mother?"

"I don't believe she did. I don't ever remember seeing her until long after your mother had died. I remember the day she came to the Citadel, it was almost a year later."

Maybe that siren was wrong...

"Where were you?"

"What?" The King tilted his head and stared at his daughter through his tears.

"When Mom got killed. Where were you?"

He took a deep breath and looked at Nessie, "down at the beach with the council. None of us knew anything until we heard the screams."

Nessie stepped forward. "Your daughter deserves to remember. Even if it's to remember who killed her."

The King nodded.

Aidina stepped close and took his hand in hers.

"I want to remember everything," she said.

He half-smiled and looked back at Nessie,

"You went to the right one for that."

CHAPTER 7

What the Water
Remembers

The chamber was ancient. It was older than the Citadel, carved of deep stone, and lined with kelp that shimmered in unnatural currents. The Moon Pool at its center glowed faintly blue, and symbols flickered in the air above it like falling embers.

Aidina stood barefoot at its edge.

Nessie knelt by the pool, her long hands tracing runes into the water. "This will feel like drowning," she said softly. "But I promise, it's how the memories return."

Aidina nodded. "I'm ready."

Behind her, the Vampire King stood in shadow. Rahlin was absent, at her request. If these were her memories, she wanted to see them alone.

Nessie pressed her fingers to Aidina's temples.

"What the water forgets," Nessie whispered, "it also remembers. What it buries, it reveals. Sink, Aidina. Remember."

And at that moment, the water rose.

Aidina opened her eyes to find herself... small again.

Eight years old. Curled against soft sea-silk sheets, her mother's voice wrapping around her like a current. Aleese smelled like ocean wind and jasmine, her dark hair cascading down her back.

"The sea sings to those who listen," Queen Aleese murmured, brushing Aidina's hair. "You are both tide and shadow, little one. You will be loved. You will be feared. But you will never be alone."

The room shimmered.

And time pulled forward.

Another memory flashed into her mind:

The air was cold. The halls of the Phantom Citadel echoed with a strange silence.

Aidina crept into the corridor, a candle trembling in her hand. "Mama?" she whispered.

She turned the corner and froze.

The siren stood before her. Wings spread wide, face blank, eyes gleaming with unnatural light.

And behind it... a shape in the darkness. Tall. Cloaked in shadow.

But their eyes glowed bright blue.

The siren lunged.

Aleese appeared in a blast of sea-magic, wind swirling around her as she screamed Aidina's name. The Queen struck the siren mid-air, and the two collided against the wall in a crash of salt and magic.

"RUN!" Aleese shouted.

But Aidina didn't.

She watched as her mother raised both arms and cast a protection spell around her, a miniature ocean glowing and weeping.

Aleese turned to the figure in the dark and said one word:

"Traitor."

And then the siren struck her from behind.

Aleese fell.

Blood bloomed like ink in water.

Her mother crawled toward her as the siren went for its final blow, but not to the queen, to Aidina.

Aleese's hands raised as a spell fell from her lips.

Aidina screamed as her world turned white.

And then all was quiet.

The beach was lit with moonlight. Waves whispered secrets on the shore.

Aidina, now sixteen, laughed as she tossed a pebble toward the sea. Rahlin, taller than she remembered, caught it mid-air with a grin.

"If you're trying to scare off selkies, you're failing," he teased.

"Well, all I know is I'm not scared of you," she said, and leaned closer. "I never was."

Their hands brushed, and there was a pause.

He looked at her, *really looked*, and whispered, "You're more sea than storm now."

She smiled, kissed his lips softly, and took his hand. Together, they walked into the surf.

The water parted for them like an old friend.

That night, they swam until dawn. She remembered admiring his true selkie form and realizing that he always saw her for who she truly was. As she swam in peace with her eyes closed, savoring the happiness felt, her mind leapt again.

Aidina opened her eyes.

She stood on the beach. The same one where she had laughed with Rahlin.

The waves were red now.

Someone was speaking softly behind her. Familiar, soft, and feminine.

She turned and saw *herself*. Kneeling. Bleeding. A blade protruding from her ribs.

Her breath came in short gasps.

Across from her... a shadow fled across the sands. A shiny flicker reflected off the sun.

And in the foreground,

Rahlin.

Frozen. Staring. Eyes wide with horror.

He took a step forward. "Aidina?"

She looked up at him. "I'm cold," she whispered.

He dropped to his knees, tried to reach her, but his hands shook, trembling.

"I didn't," he choked. "No... no..."

Then she heard another voice.

Soft. Ancient.

"Sleep, seal-boy. Forget."

A glow. A hand to Rahlin's brow.

His body convulsed. She watched him suffer as her eyes began to shut. And again, everything went dark.

Aidina shot up from the water, gasping.

The chamber was silent.

Tears streamed down her face. Her mother's voice still echoed in her ears. Her blood still clung to her skin in memory.

Her father was already beside her, helping her up.

Nessie's face was pale. "You saw it."

Aidina nodded. "She died to protect me. And someone else... someone tried to kill me with the siren next. They had bright blue eyes."

Behind them, the doors burst open.

Rahlin staggered in, eyes wide, sweat pouring down his face.

"Aidina," he rasped, "I... I saw you. The beach. I saw you die."

She turned to him.

"I remember," she whispered. "You were there."

He collapsed to his knees. "I didn't touch you. I swear. I saw someone, someone fleeing with blood on their hands."

Aidina knelt with him.

"I know you didn't. I saw. But someone also stole from you," she said.

It was someone she knew. Someone who knew her. Someone with those haunting blue eyes.

Aidina's breath caught in her throat.

Bright blue eyes in the dark.

The figure controlling the siren hadn't spoken, but now, in the silence that followed the memory, she could still hear the voice, *low, commanding, and cruel.* It was whispering to Rahlin, "Sleep, seal-boy. Forget."

But that wasn't the only voice she could still hear. The one from the beach. It belonged to someone familiar. Someone who wore *her* face?

And her mother...

Aleese hadn't screamed for help. She hadn't begged for mercy.

She had faced the figure and called them one word:

"Traitor."

Which meant she had known them.

Aidina rose slowly to her feet, shivering despite the warmth of the chamber. "The one who sent the siren... they were inside the Citadel. My mother knew them."

Nessie and the Vampire King listened to Aidina describe everything she saw. She couldn't quite piece it together when she got to the details on the beach, where she saw herself, and the reflective light leaving the beach, but she kept returning to those bright blue eyes.

Nessie frowned. "I don't know of anyone with blue eyes like that. Not here."

The Vampire King, stone-faced and silent all this time, spoke in a low voice. "Neither do I. That presence... doesn't match anyone I've ever sensed or seen in the Citadel."

But Aidina's heart was no longer unsure.

She turned to Rahlin, whose breathing had steadied beside her.

"We need to find them," she said. "Whoever they are. They were in the halls that night. They controlled the siren. I fear they were there again when I died."

Rahlin nodded slowly, his voice hoarse. "And they're still out there. Waiting."

Together, they looked toward the mouth of the chamber.

The sea would give them answers, or more ghosts.

But one thing was sure: they wouldn't stop until they found the traitor.

Rahlin and Aidina left to see what they could find in one of the many libraries. Nessie and the King stood with each other, pondering their newfound discoveries.

"We need to tell the council, Your Majesty."

"Since when do you call me that?"

"Is that not who you are? Are you not the one true King of this haunted place?" Nessie laughed softly to herself.

The King looked at his friend and put his strong hand on her shoulder,

"When are you going to get out of this skin? It's unbecoming."

"Please believe me when I say I do not enjoy it either. But the council does not meet where my true form can be shown, so the skin stays."

"She is headstrong. She is finding out more about this place than any of us seems to know. Curious, isn't it?"

"Very."

Beneath the Citadel, behind the same panel where she had found the book about her father's lost name, Aidina and Rahlin discovered another hidden alcove.

Inside was a chest covered in sea-salt rust. It held something old and fragile, a diary wrapped in velvet, sealed with wax, bearing a forgotten sigil.

They opened it.

"I was the first daughter. The first to sing to the sea. But then she was born with hair like mine, and a voice like mine, but she was more loved. More watched. More praised. I thought I would die of it. Until the witch came..."

Each page bled deeper into madness.

"She showed me how to unmake her. To become the only one. My mother wept, but I didn't care anymore. Not after what I saw."

"Tonight, I will take it all."

"First daughter?" Aidina breathed. "My *sister*?"

As she turned back a few pages, she saw a name she had never recognized: "Selianne?"

And at that moment, a crash sounded above.

The Citadel shook. Screams echoed down the marble corridors.

"Visitors?" Rahlin asked grimly.

Aidina clenched the diary. "And it does not sound like they're not here for diplomacy."

CHAPTER 8

The Forgotten Flame

They left the dank library and ran to the doors of the castle.

The Citadel gates groaned open as armored beasts crossed the marsh.

Six envoys from foreign kingdoms dismounted under banners frayed by salt and time. Their armor bore sigils of sky, stone, fire, tide, dragons, stormbirds, and forgotten things. With them came warnings.

"Darkness seeps into our wells," said the Phoenix Emissary. "Our sun fails to rise on time."

"Spells misfire," said the Storm Queen's son. "The water brings back echoes of the dead."

"The Citadel," one envoy declared, "is the eye of the storm."

They demanded an audience with the Vampire King and his wife.

Aidina sat tensely in the War Hall, the envoys cloaked in mystery and fear around her. And then: silk footsteps.

Visandra arrived, gliding like dusk through snow. Her feathers, woven into her black gown, gleamed faintly. Her smile never touched her eyes.

"I was in prayer," she lied, taking the King's arm. "Forgive my absence."

Aidina flinched.

She could *feel* the lie in Visandra's voice. And so could Rahlin, seated just behind her, watchful, tense.

The envoys bowed begrudgingly, and the council began. The Vampire King requested with his eyes that his daughter make herself scarce, but Aidina was already rising, clutching the diary she now carried like a relic of her very soul.

With Rahlin not far behind, she quickened her pace down the hall so that she could find Nessie. She saw Nessie in the garden from the window. They ran now. Trying to catch her. In her presence, they explained what they found and read the diary together.

Today, I taught Aidina to call the fish with her voice. She giggled when the minnows danced between her fingers. Father says we are the daughters of the tide, and we must always watch over one another. I believe him. She is my little moonlight, my shadow twin. Wherever she goes, I will follow.

Based on all the early entries, Selianne had once been the sunniest voice in the Citadel. Elders remembered her golden laugh, the protective way she shielded Aidina from stern tutors, the stories she spun from seashells and starlight. She had been the older sister who never let go of her sibling's hand.

But the entries changed.

There's a woman who comes in the water when no one else is there. She has feathers in her hair and eyes that change like waves. She taught me how to shape water like glass today. She says I am more powerful than my parents know. More deserving than Aidina.

Aidina smiled today, and I hated her. I don't know why. I imagined pushing her into the deep until her smile broke.

The woman says they never wanted me, that I was just a convenience, a ghost in their home. I believe her now. She looks like a swan when she flies, so elegant. She told me I could be that if I let her in.

The handwriting became erratic.

She touches my head when I sleep. I see things. I feel fire behind my eyes. Aidina is stealing them from me, stealing my parents. I must stop her.

The siren will do it. I just have to give her the song. The woman will help. She always helps. I don't want to feel this way, but the only way to end the screaming is to make it stop.

And then, a blank page.

Nessie began pacing, her voice tightening.

"Two years ago, a girl washed up near the salt cliffs below the Citadel. She was broken and raving. Kept saying she was the King's daughter. That her name was gone. We locked her away after she attacked and killed a young mermaid who tried to help her. She screamed that we had 'taken everything away'."

"I remember that," Rahlin said, his voice strained. "The mermaid's name was Laera. She was just a healer. I'd brought her to treat a fever in the barracks, and that's when it happened. She was attacked in the water, and the one who attacked her just started rambling off nonsense about being the King's daughter. I thought it was just madness. I told myself it *had* to be madness."

"No." Nessie's eyes narrowed. "It was memory theft. Whoever cast it didn't want anyone to *believe* her, even if she told the truth."

She stepped closer, lowering her voice. "Aidina...I can assure you no one on the council recalls the King and Queen ever having another daughter. Not even me. And I've known the King longer than anyone alive. But now, fragments are surfacing. Little things. The way he always looked... *grieved*, even in your happiest years. The rooms that were always locked. The vague rules about you not venturing to the eastern towers."

Rahlin tensed beside her. "You're saying someone erased her from *everyone's* minds?"

Nessie nodded, slowly.

"This isn't simple memory magic. This is an ancient, parasitic enchantment. For someone to alter the minds of the entire royal court, the leaders of each sea-born race, and *me*." Her voice cracked slightly. "They would have to be the most powerful magical beings in the land. And much older than the Citadel itself."

Aidina's stomach dropped.

"She said... in the diary..." she hesitated, then opened it, flipping to a worn page, "The witch she met was a shapeshifter. A swan. She didn't give her a name, just a song. A song she couldn't stop hearing."

"A swan," Nessie echoed. "Visandra?"

Aidina swallowed. "It's not possible, is it? I didn't think Visandra was that old, and Father doesn't remember seeing her before the day she arrived at the Citadel. But it could also be something else. Something is either hiding behind her and using her...or Visandra has been orchestrating this madness this whole time."

"He doesn't remember seeing Visandra as she is now. She may have looked very different if she's a shapeshifter, which all swan maidens are." Nessie explained.

Aidina felt her pulse thunder in her ears. "So we locked up the only witness we had. My sister."

"And let the one possibly responsible stay by the King's side," Nessie murmured.

The three of them stood in tense silence.

Then Nessie reached for Aidina's hand. At this point, Nessie decided it was time to pay the prison another visit, and Aidina agreed.

"Whatever we find below... you're not going in alone."

Rahlin nodded. "We face it together. No more shadows."

Aidina met their eyes, bracing herself against the tide of uncertainty. She closed the diary and slipped it into her cloak.

The air was cold and heavy, thick with salt and magic that hummed through the stone. Crystalline moss clung to the walls, glowing faintly in shades of blue and violet, illuminating the sealed cavern where no sunlight had touched in years.

Nessie stood guard near the reinforced coral gate, her expression unreadable. Behind her, in a prison of translucent coral and rune-marked crystal, the siren sat chained and watching. Her scales had dulled over the years, but her eyes were still sharp, and her presence was far from broken.

As Aidina stepped forward, the siren's eyes flicked toward her. She didn't flinch. She didn't growl.

She *smiled*.

"She remembers," the siren murmured, voice like the hush of waves against shore.

Nessie's eyes flickered at those words. Her mind started to race, searching memories locked away all this time. She decided to walk with Aidina to the very next cell.

As the siren silently watched them, two more figures emerged from the echoing corridor behind. It was Queen Ylla and Madrelle. Their arrival sent a ripple through the air.

"We came as soon as we felt the ward shift," said Madrelle, her eyes sharp with concern. "We felt you near the cell."

"And we heard the siren speak your name," added Ylla, her voice edged with an ancient tremor.

"She remembers me," Aidina said softly, "but she's not the only one. There's another. She's here, in the adjoining cell."

Madrelle's brow furrowed. "The mad girl?"

"Yes," Nessie murmured. "The one we locked away. She killed a young mermaid healer two years ago. She never answered to any name. And we... we didn't ask questions."

Aidina turned to the leaders, heart pounding.

"Why didn't any of you tell me this before? Didn't you recognize her?"

Madrelle and Queen Ylla were shocked and turned to Nessie with genuine confusion.

"Because," said Madrelle slowly, "I don't know her. How would I recognize someone I've never met? At that time, she was a murderous criminal who needed to be locked away. Rambling on about being the King's daughter after you had already died and come back."

Aidina's mouth went dry.

"Blind or not, I do not know this girl either. Voices are my recognition, and I've never heard hers," Ylla stated, her blind eyes shimmering in the lights.

The siren behind the bars laughed, a soft, echoing sound full of sorrow.

"She's clever, that witch," the siren crooned. "She weaves memory like thread. Plucks out what doesn't serve her purpose. Leaves you hollow and obedient."

"You mean the shapeshifting witch?" Aidina asked. "The one who looks like a swan?"

The siren's eyes glittered. "She gave your *sister* a new name. A new *truth*. And fed her lies until her heart forgot how to love."

It was at that exact moment that Madrelle felt a sudden rush in her head,

"Something in my mind just clicked. I see fragments now. A child with eyes like yours. A girl who danced with waves and sang lullabies with her sister on the beach. But it's faint. Faint like a dream I never lived."

Queen Ylla felt the same. Memories that felt like they weren't hers. She hadn't seen the girl, but she remembered her voice. At one point, she sang with both the mermaids and the sirens.

Aidina could see them all remembering at once,

"Do *you* remember the witch?"

The three fell silent.

"I don't," said Ylla, shaken. "Something I *should* remember but can't."

Madrelle's voice dropped. "Something older than the Citadel. A shadow with no name."

Nessie put a hand to her forehead. Her fingers trembled.

"I'm the Loch Ness Monster," she said aloud to herself. "I've seen kings rise and fall. I remember wars from a thousand tides ago. My clan dealt in memory magic long before this Citadel took its first breath. But this... I don't remember a girl with your eyes. I don't remember a sister. And that *terrifies me*."

"Getting glimpses of her now, at the time of uncovering her truth, feels like a trap set long ago," Madrelle said as she clenched her fists.

Aidina exhaled shakily. "Then it's true. Whoever is behind this has rewritten us. Rewritten *me*."

She looked to the siren, whose smile faded into silence.

"I need to speak with her," Aidina said. "My sister."

Ylla nodded slowly. "You have our blessing."

Madrelle placed a hand over the crystal, binding the cell. "And our protection."

Nessie didn't speak for a moment. Then she placed her hand over Aidina's heart.

"If we are to fix this... we must be prepared to remember everything. Even the pain."

Aidina nodded.

Then they turned, stepping through the passageway to the adjoining cell, where the past awaited them, locked behind eyes that had once watched her with sisterly love.

The air was thick with seawater and memory.

Torches cast flickering shadows along the cavern walls as the five of them stood before the cell. Inside, Selianne sat barefoot on the stone floor, her gown tattered, her black and silver hair falling in wild waves around her pale face. Her eyes, so like Aidina's, lifted when the group entered. And then she smiled.

"Aidina," she whispered, almost reverent. "You're alive. Alive and awake. Pity."

The group paused, tense. Nessie narrowed her eyes.

"You *remember* her?" Nessie asked.

Selianne nodded slowly, eyes never leaving her sister. "She's *mine*. My twin flame. My tether. My better half and my worst nightmare. I could never forget. No matter how many times it was taken from me."

Aidina took a step forward, hand trembling. "Who are you?"

Selianne's expression didn't falter. "I'm what's left."

Nessie motioned the others to step back. "We'll give you two a moment."

As they withdrew, the barrier of sea-glass shimmered faintly, parting at Aidina's touch. She entered.

Selianne stood now, barefoot on cold stone. "You remember me, don't you?"

Aidina's voice cracked. "No. I only remember flickers of happiness. And none of it includes you. But I remember the beach. I remember dying. I remember Mother's blood. And I remember someone watching. Someone with blue eyes."

Selianne laughed softly, a hollow sound. "She was beautiful, wasn't she? Mother. Beauty and power wrapped into one. And I snuffed her out like a God. The Swan Witch. She made everything so clear."

Aidina flinched. "*You* killed our mother."

Selianne tilted her head. "She was in the way. She saved you when I almost had you. That night, when we were children. She gave her life and her magic to keep you safe, to make you forget. I hated her for that."

"You were my sister."

"I *am* your sister!" Selianne shouted suddenly, eyes glowing with emotion. "But you took everything. Their love. The throne. The light. I *was* first."

Tears welled in Aidina's eyes. "So you waited. Waited until my sixteenth birthday, when I was happy. In love. When no one suspected."

Selianne's voice dropped, chilling. "I watched you from the cliff that night. I followed you to the beach. I saw your joy, and I ended it. You looked so surprised when the blade entered. I thought I'd feel powerful. But all I felt... was nothing."

Aidina stepped back. "You *murdered* me."

"You were already dead to me," Selianne whispered. "She made sure of that."

Aidina turned, her face pale. She stepped from the cell and slammed the barrier back into place. Her hands were shaking. Nessie caught her before she fell, the weight of the truth too much.

"The prophecy should have stopped with me. But then came *you*."

"Prophecy?"

The Vampire King stood in his crimson and black war robes in his chambers before the mirror. His stormy eyes were fixed on the door's reflection as Visandra swept in, her swan-feathered cloak trailing behind her.

"You were gone," he said, voice like a blade.

"I was in my chambers," she replied evenly, though her gaze never quite met his.

"For days? During the chaos? While our daughter…" He turned slowly, scarlet eyes glowing.

Visandra's expression tightened. "Your daughter."

He stepped closer. "*Our* daughter, by marriage if not by blood. Do not play semantics, Visandra."

"You hide things from me," she said, voice rising. "You never trusted me. Not truly. You've always loved Aleese."

The King's jaw clenched. "*That* was *never* a secret. She died because someone we trusted betrayed her. Betrayed *me*."

Visandra's eyes gleamed. "And you still don't remember who?"

"No," he growled. "And that's the most terrifying part. The witch's magic erased more than names; it stole *truth*."

Visandra paced, agitated. "And why did you marry me? Were you ever in love with me, or was it just for power?"

He froze. "Speak carefully, woman. You think you have me cornered. You think that because you know my name, you have power over me. I am not some demon pet, Visandra, you do not control me, and you do not control this Citadel."

Her lips curled slightly. "You were *never* supposed to have a daughter. The prophecy was clear. And yet you defied it. Aleese gave you that…" She stopped short.

The Vampire King's eyes narrowed. "You will watch your tongue, *witch*. That prophecy can drown in the same sea where I found you."

Visandra turned away.

"Do not walk away from *me*, Visandra. You think I don't remember how you arrived here? Bleeding in my waters. Begging for my help. Promising to fix what you knew you couldn't. I know what you were sent for."

Silence stretched between them.

She finally spoke softly, "You were right to fear the blue eyes."

CHAPTER 9

The Pages We Fear to Turn

The moonlight wove silver threads across the Citadel as Aidina stood beside Nessie on the quiet balcony of the north wing. The sea in the distance shimmered, indifferent to the chaos below its waves. Aidina clutched the diary of her forgotten sister to her chest, her fingers trembling.

"There's something that's been bothering me," she said at last. "That prophecy my sister mentioned. Have you heard it before? Do you know what it is?"

Nessie tilted her head, her lake-colored eyes reflecting the starlight. "I've heard many prophecies in my time. From selkie seers, from kelp witches in the trench. But this one..." She paused. "No. Not once. And it doesn't seem like anyone knows the words."

Aidina hesitated, then said, "I didn't mention something. Something I overheard a few nights ago."

Nessie turned, attentive.

"It was late. I was walking through the hall beneath the king's chambers. I didn't mean to eavesdrop, but... Visandra and my father were arguing."

She drew a shaky breath.

"She said something. She said it angrily, carelessly. She said she knew his name. His real name."

Nessie's eyes snapped toward her. "Are you sure?"

Aidina nodded.

"But that's not possible," Nessie whispered. "That spell erased his name from every record, every mind in the Citadel. No one here should remember it."

"I don't even know it," Aidina said bitterly. "And he doesn't either. But he knows that he doesn't know it."

Nessie was quiet for a long time. The wind rustled her hair like kelp in the tide.

"I remember his name," she said softly. "I was away, visiting the selkies in the north, when the spell took hold. You wouldn't know it, my dear. You were born in the Citadel while the spell still applies. And because no one remembers it, neither he nor anyone else could say it to you."

Aidina's eyes widened. "Then she shouldn't know it, should she?"

"No," Nessie said. "She shouldn't."

They stared at each other in the moonlight, realization pooling between them like a rising tide.

"If she knows his name," Nessie said slowly, "she too was not here when the spell was cast."

"And she knew him *before*," Aidina finished.

The implications made her stomach twist.

"But, she won't be able to say it. The spell prevents it. I could say it to you now, and you would either not hear it or you wouldn't understand what I said." Nessie explained.

"Try it."

Nessie looked at her, intrigued by her curiosity, and formed the words,

"Your father ◇◇◇◇◇◇◇, The Vampire King of the Phantom Citadel"

Aidina put her head down in defeat. She had no idea, so she decided to move the conversation along.

"That would mean she was close to him, personally, before he ever became king and before anyone even knew who he was," Nessie said. "But no one knows that story. It was always... foggy."

Aidina thought of the vague explanations. Of Visandra's elegance, her evasions. She always claimed to have met the Vampire King "at court" but never said which one.

"She never told me how they met," Aidina whispered. "She never told *anyone.*"

Nessie stood slowly, her expression darkening. "If she knew him before the spell... it means she either helped cast it and it didn't extend to her, or was protected by someone who did and made to leave the Citadel so that it didn't touch her then."

Aidina felt her skin prickle. "Maybe she heard it from someone outside of the Citadel?"

"That is a possibility. It only can't be said *here.*"

"But who could do a spell like that? Because they did the same thing to Selianne."

"It's time we start digging into the truth, Aidina. I am starting to think Visandra might not be the mastermind. But she's far from innocent. She might be a puppet. Of a darker hand." Her expression darkened. "Like a Black Swan Maiden."

Aidina froze. "Those are only myths."

"Not myths. Histories scrubbed clean," Nessie replied. "Twisted maidens, once pure of heart, warped by ancient magic. It rots them from the soul outward. Leaves their eyes glowing blue like frostbitten skies."

Aidina swallowed the knot in her throat.

"In all my time brokering peace, I've only come across whispers of one. Their magic is very ancient and very powerful. It pulls directly from the shadows. I believe that is what we are up against now."

"We need to speak to my father."

The Vampire King's study smelled of dust and forgotten ink. A single candle flickered on the desk as the trio entered. He looked up, weary eyes gleaming crimson.

"You've learned something," he said before they could speak.

Nessie stepped forward gently. "There may be something in your late mother's diary. Something you may not have seen."

He hesitated. "I couldn't bring myself to read it all, so you could be correct in that regard. I always stop after the joy of those first entries... but I always think about it when I'm missing my brothers."

"There's something else," Aidina said softly. "Someone."

She met his eyes.

"You had another daughter. Before me."

The air in the room thickened like mist rolling in from a graveyard.

The Vampire King blinked, unmoving. "What did you say?"

Nessie took out the dusty old diary, its cover cracked, the leather dried like forgotten skin. She placed it on his table.

"We found this. Hidden in the archives beneath the scriptorium. It's hers. Your first daughter. Her name was Selianne."

He didn't move. His face was stone, but his hands trembled.

"She wrote of you," Aidina continued. "Of our mother. Of me. She loved me. Looked after me. Then something changed."

"This can't be possible."

Nessie opened the diary to the first few pages. They were light, playful, and full of hope. He read slowly, his eyes narrowing as if peering into the fog of a dream.

"...she called you 'Papa,'" Aidina said. "Said you used to bring her blood-orchid nectar when she was ill. Said she wanted to protect me."

The King's eyes glazed with something more profound than grief. He pressed his fingertips to his temples.

"I..." he whispered. "I... remember a girl. She wore her mother's ring on a chain...black and silver hair in waves..." He shut his eyes. "But it ends there. I thought she was a dream I once had. I thought it was part of the grief after Aleese died."

"She was real," Nessie said gently. "And she was stolen from all our memories."

The King looked up slowly. "How?"

"We think it happened the night Aidina died," Nessie said. "The day the Black Swan Maiden touched her was the day everyone forgot her."

"She was manipulated," Aidina added. "Drawn into darkness. Twisted until she hated all of us. It wasn't her fault."

The King stared at the diary. When he spoke, his voice was low, ragged. "I failed her."

"You were made to," Nessie said.

"Hold. Black Swan Maiden? Those are myths. And she can't be *my* daughter."

"All of these things are confusing but intertwined. She spoke of a prophecy." Nessie explained as she shut the book.

"She's still alive?"

"A prisoner. She was the girl who murdered the mermaid healer two years ago on the beach. The one that rambled."

Aidina watched her father's eyes flicker with confusion and re-membrance.

"She said the prophecy stopped with her, but then I came."

The Vampire King remembered his previous encounter with Visandra. But he kept it to himself, at least for now.

With trembling hands, he opened his mother's diary once more. The first pages spoke of love. Of birth. Of laughter in the tides. Then... a change. Unease. Dreams that weren't her own. A figure with blue eyes whispering promises. Magic laced in nightmares.

"This is how it began," Nessie murmured, looking over the text with him. "The same spiral Selianne followed."

"They were both marked," Aidina whispered. "Just at different times."

Meanwhile, in the shadows of the east wing, Rahlin stood in front of Visandra's door. She had summoned him with no expla-nation. As he stepped inside, her silhouette stood at the window, moonlight staining her white robes with cold brilliance.

"You're a curious little selkie," she said softly, not turning. "And a loyal one."

"I heard what the siren said," Rahlin said. "And what the girl in the cell confessed."

Visandra finally turned. Her eyes glimmered like the outside sea. "Then you know you are nothing more than a piece on a board none of us can see."

Rahlin's throat tightened.

"You were chosen," she said, stepping closer, "not for strength. But for obedience. You care too much. *That* is your weakness."

"I protect Aidina," he said, firm.

Her smile was cold. "Then protect her from the truth, if you can."

She reached out and touched his temple. A pulse of searing magic slammed into him. His eyes widened. Light, blue, and flooded his vision.

And he screamed.

The library no longer felt like a sanctuary in the damp corridors beneath the Citadel.

Aidina and Nessie left her father's chambers. They had filled his mind with more information than he could handle at one time. And they stood before a tall, dust-laced shelf hidden behind a false wall in the Citadel's west wing. It was a wing that hadn't been touched since her father's coronation.

Nessie remembered it: a chamber used by the queen consort before she died, the queen who had once been *only* a swan maiden.

The air was thick with cobwebs and old magic. Aidina lit a crystal lantern, its glow throwing long shadows across the room as Nessie traced her fingers along the spines of ancient texts.

"Here," Nessie said, pulling free a tome bound in leather that had faded to the gray of dried bone. The title shimmered faintly.

"The Mourning Feather: Histories of the Swan and the Sea."

She laid it open between them. The pages were handwritten in a language only half-familiar, but the drawings, ethereal women with wings for arms and eyes glowing in starlight, told part of the tale.

Nessie whispered as she translated:

"There were once twelve high swan maidens who served the old world's magic. They were guardians of memory and purity, able to move between forms, between lakes and skies and dreams. But one among them... was cast out."

Her finger stopped on an illustration. A swan with feathers going dark at the tips. Its wings dipped in shadow, a crown of bones above its head.

Aidina stared. "That one? That's her?"

Nessie nodded. "The first Black Swan Maiden."

"She began to twist. First emotionally. Her grief curdled into anger. She fed on human suffering, love turned to jealousy, memories stolen and rewritten. She lost her name, but gained something else, power beyond the others. Forbidden spells. Thought-speech. Shape-shifting."

Aidina leaned closer, heart pounding.

Nessie continued:

"Her favorite form was that of a pale swan with a silver beak. She was seen near the mirrored marshes... planting memories in the minds of maidens she marked. Turning them into vessels."

Aidina looked up sharply. "That's where Visandra was raised. The mirrored marshes. She told me once, when she was *actually* being nice to me. Said it was where the air sang with silence."

The book seemed to groan beneath their hands. Nessie flipped another page, revealing an inked, rough, but unmistakable portrait.

A woman with long white hair, eyes hollow and bright as stars, a faint crown woven of shadowed reeds on her brow.

Aidina felt her breath catch. "Is that her? The witch Selianne wrote about? It has to be. The one who twisted her. The shapeshifter."

Nessie nodded grimly. "And I think she twisted Visandra, too."

Silence stretched between them, as if the room itself recoiled from the truth.

"To bend anyone to her will, the Black Swan didn't have to steal them. Just touch them. Implant a dream and a fear. And over time, that seed would grow. They would forget what they were or who they were and start to believe they belonged to the darkness instead."

"She's been controlling Visandra for years," Aidina whispered. "Maybe since before she ever met my father."

"She likely introduced them," Nessie said. "Groomed Visandra to charm him. To gain power through marriage."

"But it's so odd. My father never said how they met. I do remember when she came; I was old enough for that. Which means Selianne also remembers. We all agree it was about a year later. But she did come in like she had been there for years."

"It is so odd. If Visandra had known your father before the spell, I would have known her too. But I don't. I don't remember anything about her before the wedding."

"Face it, Nessie. Your mind has been messed with, too."

They stood in the cold quiet of that room, surrounded by books that had nearly forgotten their own words.

Nessie's voice, low and solemn:

"We're not just fighting a sorceress. We're fighting a ghost, a parasite who has been stealing her way into bloodlines for centuries."

Aidina closed the book with trembling hands.

"Then it's time to burn the rot out of the roots.

CHAPTER 10

The Poison Beneath

Screams filled the night. Aidina felt life being sucked out of the Citadel. There was no happiness, not anymore. The screams ran in her ears, but she was imagining them. She heard the cries of the past. Did she not?

The Vampire King's steed's body was found at dawn.

It had collapsed on the marble steps leading to the Citadel's northern wing, its white fur blackened and clinging to its ribs like ash. Blood slicked the stones, but there were no wounds; it was just a scorched brand seared over its heart. A twisted sigil Aidina didn't recognize. The creature's eyes were wide open, glassy with terror, and its legs were twisted unnaturally, as if it had died mid-flight.

When the servants found it, they screamed. When the Vampire King saw it, he fell to one knee and clutched his chest, his face graying.

Aidina reached him just in time, calling for Rahlin and Nessie. He didn't speak, just stared at the mark burned into the steed's hide as his breathing grew shallower, his fingers trembling over the place where his own heart beat.

Later that night, the Citadel was quiet, but not with peace. Whispers spread like rot through the marble halls: citizens were vanishing.

At first, there were a few; a kelpie child never returned from the well-spring, and a siren scout failed to report from the western gate. Then the numbers grew.

Dozens were gone. Entire families. Their homes left as if they'd simply stepped out for a walk, food half-eaten, lamps still glowing, doors unlocked. The Citadel's pulse slowed with dread.

The war council convened in secret beneath the Whispering Chamber. Visandra's absence was noted by all, and spoken of by none.

Madrelle, the Siren leader, was the first to speak. "The king weakens. The people vanish. There is rot within our walls."

Nessie nodded, arms crossed. "Something old is stirring. The magic twisting through this place is not just residual, it's active. Intelligent."

The Siren Leader leaned forward. "The spell that's feeding on our king and killing our people, it's not from outside. It's inside. Someone's anchoring it here."

"Visandra," Aidina whispered.

Heads turned. Silence fell.

"She didn't arrive until almost a year after my mother died," she continued. "But it was assumed she had come to help. What if she didn't?"

Nessie added quietly, "Selianne never mentioned Visandra in her diary. Not once."

"But what if she did?" Aidina rose. "We assumed she meant someone else."

"There is still much information we don't know, Princess. But we must hasten to find out before we lose your father and the Citadel as a whole." Madrelle replied, her eyes full of anger and fear.

They descended into the cell again, the air cold and crackling. Selianne sat cross-legged on the stone, her hair matted, her lips chapped, but her eyes were clear.

"You've come again," she said, smiling faintly. "To remember me?"

"Selianne," Aidina asked softly, "do you know the name Visandra?"

Selianne laughed. A dry, bitter sound. "Do I *know* her? She came after the witch twisted me. The woman in white with a swan's eyes. She whispered things. Told me my parents never loved me. Told me you hated me. She fed the fire already burning."

"So her name *was* Visandra?" Nessie asked.

Selianne nodded slowly. "That's what the black-winged thing called her."

A shadow flickered through the torchlight in the hall.

"She wasn't real," Selianne continued. "Not at first. But she became real. And now she's the Queen."

Aidina swallowed. "Became real...?"

"She was gone. She was in between worlds," Selianne murmured. "Long before the wedding. Long before the throne."

"In between? What are you talking about?"

"She was between this place and another. She was fighting herself every day, but her true self was not the one that was winning. The black witch did that." Selianne laughed.

A silence fell. The poison had roots. Roots deeper than any of them knew.

Selianne exhaled. "You've come to ask if I regret it."

"Yes," Aidina said.

Selianne met her eyes. "I don't. I regret not doing it sooner."

There was no hate in her voice. No fire. Just quiet clarity. The calm of someone whose mind had been drowned for too long to know the truth from the shadow.

The council reconvened in hushed horror, but Aidina stayed. She wanted a truly private audience with her sister. Maybe she was so cold to her because there were people around. Maybe her tone would be different if she were really alone.

Aidina stood outside Selianne's cell alone.

The torchlight flickered against damp stone walls. The heavy door creaked as she pushed it open. Inside, her sister sat on the stone bench, legs crossed, black veins spider-webbing beneath her skin. Her once-bright eyes were now dim, tinged with a sickly violet.

"You're *still* here," Selianne said, rolling her eyes.

Aidina nodded. She couldn't speak at first.

"You always wanted to be the hero, didn't you? Even now, trying to save the dying villain."

Aidina's voice cracked. "Why, Selianne?"

Her sister smiled, teeth stained dark.

"Because no one else would. Because they all loved you more. Because I saw what the Black Swan showed me. She told me the truth: we were never meant to share the same throne."

"Why are you so sure that I wanted it? You were older than I. It would have been yours first. Even now, I don't want that power."

"You only *think* that."

"I *know* that. The throne offers no freedom. Freedom is what I want. It's what I *require*."

"How funny, because that is exactly what I did for our mother. *Freed* her."

"And me?"

Selianne looked away. "I failed the first time. Mother saved you. But you were always meant to die. I only regret not doing it sooner."

"How could you be so sure of these feelings? You loved me once. And I, you."

"The prophecy was clear. The darkness was stopped. And then you became the end of peace. Your birth should *never* have happened."

Aidina backed away slowly, the words burning like acid in her throat.

Selianne coughed violently, a long rattle ending in a stream of black ichor that splattered the floor. When she looked up again, her eyes were blank.

"I wanted to free you, too. Bring you into this darkness so I wouldn't be alone, and I failed."

Her head hung after that, and she was gone.

Rumors of Selianne's death spread faster than fire, but none of them knew why her body had turned to mist and bone, nor why the siren beside her had withered into near non-existence.

Before her final breath, the siren had turned to Aidina and said in a voice barely more than a sigh:

"It is not only you in danger, girl. The monster that wears the skin... need beware the shore."

That night, the Citadel pulsed with unease. Black feathers appeared in the corridors where no bird could've flown. The King grew weaker, the blood in his veins turning dark. The sigil on the dead steed still smoldered.

The war council would need to act. But first, they had to face the truth: the enemy was not outside their gates.

It was already among them.

The Vampire King had not risen from his bed in days.

Moonlight filtered through the gauze curtains, casting a spectral glow over his fevered form. Wet cloths lay strewn across the floor. His breathing was shallow and strained, and he whispered names no one recognized now and then, except, perhaps, in dreams.

Aidina sat silently at his bedside, her fingers curled tightly around the carved arm of his chair. The fire had gone out. She didn't ask for more wood.

Behind her, the door creaked open.

Visandra entered, her black and white robes trailing across the stone, eyes calm and unreadable.

"You shouldn't be here," she said softly.

"He's my father."

Visandra tilted her head. "That never seemed to matter before."

Aidina stood, the flicker of a flame catching in her eyes. "Pardon? I've always been here for my father. What exactly did you do to him?"

"I've done nothing," Visandra said, her voice clipped. "But I could ask the same of you. Since your *miraculous* return, this Citadel has been on the edge of ruin."

The silence that followed crackled like ice.

Aidina stepped forward slowly. "Citizens are disappearing. My father's horse is dead. And my father is rotting from the inside out."

"You think I had a hand in that?"

Aidina's voice was soft. Too soft. "I think you know things you shouldn't. Like his name."

Visandra froze.

"I heard you tell him you knew it. When you were fighting. No one knows his name. Not even me. Not unless they were there... before."

A breath. Then another. Then Visandra smiled, as if she had just changed into another person.

"You have no idea what you're involved in," she said, stepping close. "You're still a child, Aidina. You think this is about names and spells?"

Her hand hovered at her side, where the small swan-etched pendant always dangled.

"Your mother *also* played with magic far older than she understood. You are the daughter of a curse and a throne. And you think you're strong enough to fix all of this?"

"And how *exactly* do you know what my mother did or didn't do?"

"This will not end well for you, small one."

"I'm not afraid of you."

Visandra's eyes glinted with something ancient and unreadable. "You should be."

Then, without another word, she turned on her heel and stormed from the room.

Aidina followed her shadow to the courtyard window, watching Visandra mount her old steed and gallop into the night without a backward glance.

The Citadel watched her go, and something inside its walls seemed to sigh.

Aidina moved like someone walking underwater.

Nessie had gathered more records from the sealed libraries, muttering about old contracts made in swan blood and shadow ink. Left alone in the tower, Aidina couldn't shake the feeling that something vital was... wrong.

Not just Visandra.

Not just the Citadel.

But Rahlin. His presence had been scarce.

He'd grown cold. Detached. His eyes didn't meet hers the same way. And twice now, she'd caught him standing at odd corners, unmoving, as if listening to something far away.

When he entered the tower chamber, she was startled.

"You're late," she joked, trying to smile.

He blinked slowly. "You didn't give a time."

He looked down the scrolls Nessie had requested and handed them to her as he turned to leave.

"Rahlin," she said, stepping in front of him, her heart hammering.

He looked at her, but the weight in his gaze was wrong. Too heavy. Too hollow.

"You're acting like someone else."

"Am I?"

He touched her cheek, and then he was gone. His touch was not the same.

She stared at the door he left out of so quickly. Something was wrong, and she had no quarreling thoughts. It was definitely because of Visandra.

Nessie burst in moments later, more scrolls in hand.

"The diaries weren't all. I found a letter... from Aleese to the Queen Mother. It's mostly torn, but there's a line that froze my blood."

Aidina took the fragile parchment in her hands.

"She is beautiful, this swan woman, but her shadow arrives before she does. There is something in her reflection that doesn't belong. Maybe the friend I had all those long years ago was really gone."

"She meant Visandra?" Aidina whispered.

"I think she did. But this is when your grandfather was still reigning. Which means it is all too possible that Visandra knew your father before he lost his name, which means I could have known her as well," Nessie replied. "And Aidina... there's more."

Nessie turned over another page. "Swan maidens don't rot. They don't wither. But black swan maidens? They don't just twist, they cause rebirth. Through death. Through blood. Through *sacrifice*. That means..."

"She's not possessed," Aidina said slowly. "She's replaced?"

"Maybe Visandra is fighting a battle of her own. Between being her old self and being this new self conjured by the Black Swan Maiden."

They both went silent.

"*That* is what she meant. Selianne said that Visandra was fighting herself, but her true self was losing. *This* is what she meant. But that means that at some point, Visandra died."

"Not only that, but reborn as something evil. Maybe that is why she has such disdain for you.."

Aidina thought about it. She thought back to when Visandra told her she was a stranger.

"That's why she called *me* a stranger. Because she's one. Because I didn't return like she did."

Outside, the fog rolled deeper over the Citadel.

Visandra rode silently. Her steed galloped hard into the reed-choked wilds. Visandra leaned low over the animal's back, wind tearing through her hair, her swan pendant catching moonlight like a shard of ice.

She rode past the weeping tree near the forgotten shrine. Past the broken antler totems half-swallowed by mud. Her destination was a ruin older than the Citadel itself, an overgrown spire of blackened stone and dead vines.

Inside, the remnants of the Black Swan's altar remained.

Visandra knelt there in silence. Her fingers shook as she touched the moss-dark slab.

"Why do you still haunt me?" she whispered.

There was no answer.

Only a distant, echoing flutter, not wings. Not wind. But something that remembered flight, long ago.

CHAPTER 11

Shadows By the Sea

The salty wind tugged at Aidina's hair as she approached her favorite spot by the shore. The tide whispered against the stones, but the familiar rhythm felt hollow to her now, like the heartbeat of a place losing its soul.

Rahlin was there, seated on his driftwood where the water met the sand. His gaze was fixed on the endless, unblinking, distant blue.

"You came," he said without turning.

Aidina hesitated a moment before stepping closer. The scent of brine mixed with something darker, like sorrow or fear.

"I've been looking for you," she said softly.

He didn't reply. After a long pause, he finally spoke, voice low and rough. "The water... it doesn't sing to me anymore. I can't feel its pulse, its life. It's like the tide's stolen something from inside me."

His shoulders were tense, rigid.

"What is happening to you?" Aidina asked, stepping closer.

Rahlin's hands clenched. "I'm not sure. But it is tearing at me. Remembering things so deeply embedded in my mind that they could have disappeared. And then forgetting the most important thoughts and dreams that have ever crossed my mind.."

Aidina reached out, hesitating, then took his hand gently, the same way he had held hers years ago, before darkness crept between them.

"I see it in you," she said, voice breaking. "The changes. It scares me."

Rahlin's head turned slowly. His eyes, still that strange stormy gray, held hers. For a heartbeat, the old warmth flickered through.

"I love you, Aidina. I always have. I would never hurt you." His thumb brushed her knuckles.

Their lips met, fragile and desperate, clinging to a past slipping away.

Unseen in the shadows, Nessie watched. Her gaze sharpened, her decision clear.

When Aidina turned away and returned to the castle, Nessie stepped from the darkness and approached Rahlin.

"That was touching," she said flatly.

Rahlin stood slowly. "I know you've seen it too."

"Your magic falters. You're *fading*, Rahlin"," she said quietly, eyes narrowing. "But your heart... what are you hiding?"

Rahlin's smile was thin, but his eyes darkened with something unspoken.

"If you're being controlled, I'll free you. But if you're not... I'll end you."

The history of the Citadel was intertwined with the history of the Citizens who were present before it reached its haunted reputation. Nessie didn't trust her own mind. She knew her memories had been altered at one point, but didn't know if they had been altered again.

What she did know was that the magic that fell over this land was the only reason there was a library in the Citadel. If it wasn't a personally written diary, it was a book written by magic that documented everything that happened on the Citadel's grounds. Whether it be now or before the Citadel had existed in its true form and essence. She pulled one of the books from the shelves and started to turn the dusty pages until she found what she needed.

The Veiled Record of the Citadel

Many years before the rise of the Citadel, there had been four.

A young girl with sea-glass eyes and kelp in her hair, Aleese. A fledgling vampire boy who refused to sleep indoors. The future Vampire King. A swan maiden with laughter like chimes, Visandra. And Nessie, the changeling girl who never cried.

Nessie was almost surprised to see her name on the same line as Visandra's, but she continued reading.

They had no kingdom then. Only the ruins of old temples and a war that had nearly devoured them. They met in the in-between places: tidepools, caves, dried-up battlegrounds.

They met at the end of the first war, when the sky burned and water refused to mirror the world. Children, not yet rulers, not yet ruined.

When they grew into their older years and the second war had started to grow in the West, the Citadel welcomed the half-starved boy whose fangs hadn't fully grown in, who had been orphaned when the vampire royals were slaughtered in their sleep. The new King Cynric and Queen Rani took him in. They were of a fractured realm, and they named him son. Information Nessie knew already. She had also pulled the book where he documented his own history in the castle, so this was only confirmation.

Pushing forward, she found that Aleese fell for him *first*.

She was then a queen, barefoot, caramel-skinned, with wild dark hair and an accent that crashed like waves. Her mother ended herself the night her daughter took the crown. Aleese didn't flinch from it. She ruled the tides with laughter and steel.

He never told her he loved her. Not with words. But when she sang to the sea, he always watched. When she laughed, he tried to echo it. When she grieved, he grieved quietly.

And Visandra saw it all.

They were inseparable when they were growing up as the four: the vampire boy, the sea queen, the swan girl, and the impossible changeling, whose human form flickered like fog and whose monstrous body hid under lochs and lullabies.

They camped together in ruined watchtowers, ate berries, and spoke of old dreams. They made vows, all of them, to build something better after the war, the thing that would one day be the Citadel. They were never without each other until growing older started to mean growing separately.

Even then, something grew in Visandra.

It was not rage. Not yet. It was longing. Ache. The kind that turns the air sharp around a name.

Visandra had loved him, too, since they were children. But where Aleese was storm and flame, Visandra was air and silence. Her love was a quiet offering, feather-light, unnoticed, the kind that grows heavier the longer it's ignored.

He danced once with Visandra, under silver trees. And for a moment, she thought she had been seen.

But he spoke Aleese's name in his sleep.

Visandra wept by the lake alone. Nessie found her and tried to comfort her. But Nessie was a creature of balance, not sentiment. She warned her gently: *"You can't make someone love you by bleeding for them."*

Visandra never listened.

That night, she flew north.

This is what Nessie was looking for. She wondered how this entry was in the book for a split second but then realized that Visandra would have had to put it here. In a conversation with the Vampire King, she remembered that he said she had spent a long time down here, many days, alone.

She didn't trust her memories either. Or she didn't trust herself to remember how she got to this point, so she wrote it down.

This thought crossed Nessie's mind before, but she never imagined where Visandra would have put information like this. Now she had it, and she continued to read on.

She found her mentor: a swan maiden older than snow, said to have flown the sky before kingdoms had names. But the mentor had turned. She had seen love wither and become hatred too many times. She had devoured her own shadow to survive it.

She became the **Black Swan Maiden**, and Visandra begged her for strength.

"I don't want to hurt him," she whispered.

"You lie," the Black Swan said, stroking her cheek. "You want him to kneel."

The training began. The pain, the tearing of feathers, the stitching of songs that cracked the mind and melted resistance.

And eventually... the ritual.

Visandra died beneath the full moon, her body torn open like a prayer. When she rose again, she was not alone.

Her love had split. One half still wept for the one she loved.

The other sharpened its beak and waited for blood.

When Nessie closed the book after figuring out Visandra was split into two people, she realized the side that is the most present was the darkness that came from the ritual. The power she wanted. The other half is dormant at most moments but shines through, mostly in the presence of the one she loved so much. But that half was weak. Dying. Losing.

Going through Queen Rani's diary once more, she saw a few entries that could fit Visandra, but it could also be her mentor who kept Visandra back while she planted her dark magics.

One particular entry said:

"She was always there. Quiet, kind. But there is kindness that waits its turn like a blade waits its sheath. I should have seen her hunger. I should have known what a swan does when denied flight."

This is the only entry she needed. She decided it was time to talk to her friend. They had much to discuss. Little did she know that behind her investigation, Rahlin was doing one of his own.

Rahlin moved like a shadow through the upper archive halls, fingers inked with dusk, eyes heavy with the symbols he couldn't quite translate. Swan feathers etched into stone with spiral markings like breaking glass.

He had found too much.

And he knew.

He knew the timeline didn't fit. He found that no swan maiden, not even Visandra, could cast such total mind-control over others unless they had crossed into forbidden rites. But most of all, he knew that Queen Rani had once stood against Visandra's mentor and not Visandra herself.

Until she gave up with the death of her sons and allowed the anger to take hold of her, she let the madness whispering to her control her thoughts. She stole her son's name out of misplaced rage and shamed herself for it in the diary, but was happy about it in appearances.

Rahlin should have gone to Aidina. Instead, he stayed. Searched. *That* was his last mistake.

He was taken before dawn.

Not violently, no blood trail, no torn skin. The magic was older than that. He felt a lullaby curl into his mind like rot under his tongue. A feathered hand touched his shoulder. The world fell away. Rahlin awoke to feathers choking his mouth.

He tried to scream, but his voice had been taken. His body would not move.

The altar was stone, cold, and damp beneath him. Swan feathers pinned his arms in unnatural angles. A coppery liquid slicked the floor. The walls of the ruined chapel breathed, literally pulsed with sound. A wet heartbeat echoing not from him... but from something buried deep below.

The Black Swan Maiden stepped into view.

She did not look like death. She looked like a woman who had forgotten how to die. Her wings trailed rot, and her eyes shimmered with layers, like fish scales painted over flame.

She laid a hand on Rahlin's chest. Not roughly. With care.

"You screamed that day, too," she said softly. "When I broke them."

Visandra sat, catatonic, near the edge of the chapel. A husk in mourning. Her mouth moved with silent prayers, her hands bound in chains of gold and teeth. Her hair was knotted with dried blood.

Something inside her stirred. Something that had not been born human.

In the Citadel, the Vampire King stood, alive.

His skin no longer bruised with shadow. His eyes were clear, and the crimson in his veins stayed strong.

The council stared as he walked into his throne room without assistance.

"She's gone," one whispered. "And he thrives."

"Then perhaps she *is* the sickness."

Nessie stood at the edge of the chamber, her mouth drawn. She said nothing, though her fingers gripped the spine of the diary so tightly it left gouges.

She had read what lay at the end of it, which was the Queen Mother's final warning.

"If she returns, do not kill her. She will only be reborn worse."

"Bury her with her wings torn. Only then will the curse end."

CHAPTER 12

Shaping the Shadows

Aidina couldn't find Rahlin.

His coat still hung near his door, untouched. His scent was salt, fur, and cedar, but it had faded from the corridor with every passing hour.

She didn't panic. Not right away. But by midday, she was standing outside her father's war room with hollow eyes and trembling hands.

The Vampire King dismissed the guards before she spoke.

"He didn't leave a note," she said. "Not even a sign."

He studied her, ageless and grave. "Rahlin wouldn't leave you."

"I know." Her voice cracked. "But something has been troubling him. Hurting him."

They sat in silence, the war maps below them useless now.

"I chose him," the King said after a long pause. "Not just because he was strong. But because I saw how he looked at you. And you looked back. Like I once did... with your mother."

Aidina closed her eyes. She remembered Rahlin's hand at her back during festivals, steady as tides. The way he stood between her and anything sharp, even her own thoughts.

"He's not just my guard," she whispered.

"I know."

Meanwhile, Nessie stood before the council, flanked by flickering lamps and a pile of cracked, mildew-stained tomes from the Queen Mother's restricted archive.

"This is her," Nessie said, slapping down a faded page. "Visandra didn't rise from the dead on her own. She was brought back. Twisted."

The council murmured in growing unease. The image on the page was indistinct: wings, darkness, and a woman's figure without a face.

"The Black Swan Maiden," Nessie continued. "Name lost to time. Until now. Her name is *Elandra*."

Murmurs turned to gasps.

"And she didn't die centuries ago like the records claim. She's here. And she's been here."

Aidina burst through the chamber doors before the panic could take hold.

"Rahlin's gone," she said. "He didn't vanish, he was taken."

The chamber stilled. Nessie's mouth fell open slightly, and then she said what they were all thinking:

"She's going to use him. Just like she used Selianne."

Far away, Visandra, her crueler half at the helm, stood before a gathering of foreign leaders in a cold, starlit grove.

"The Citadel is rotting," she told them, voice like ice over glass. "Its rulers traffic in cursed bloodlines and undead poison. You've seen it. You've *felt* it. The weakening. The madness creeping through your borders."

The leaders shifted uncomfortably. One of them, a tall woman in silver war armor from the High Clans, narrowed her eyes.

"And what would you have us do?" she asked.

"War," said Visandra. "We end this now. Before it spreads."

But the silver-clad leader wrote a message in her lap with trembling hands and gave it to a cloaked rider behind her.

"Take this to the Citadel," she whispered. "Something isn't right."

Nessie and Madrelle left that same night. The Selkie Chief took to the waters, scouring the kelp beds and hidden trenches. Rahlin was one of his own; he was determined to find him. Nessie and Madrelle rode hard on horseback toward the ruined cathedral on the northern cliffs, where rumor said dark things moved at night.

They found the altar beneath the dead tree.

Rahlin was there, bound by enchanted seaweed, eyes vacant, chest barely moving. And standing over him,

Elandra.

Her true face.

No paintings had ever captured it because no eye had survived long enough to see it.

She had no eyes, only sockets full of glistening feathers, and her lips bled black ichor. Wings of bone and oil arched behind her.

"You came," she said. "Good."

Madrelle raised her staff, but Elandra's scream shattered the trees. Magic howled across the altar like wind through a corpse's mouth. Madrelle was struck through the chest and thrown into a tree. Blood bloomed through her gown.

Nessie didn't scream.

She chanted.

The most potent spell in her arsenal, the one she swore never to use again, lit up the clearing in pale violet fire. The sky cracked.

Elandra shrieked and staggered. Nessie grabbed both Madrelle and Rahlin and vanished into the mist.

Back at the Citadel, Madrelle was healed by nightfall.

But Rahlin didn't wake.

Aidina sat beside him, cold fingers brushing through his salt-matted hair. His breath came in broken waves. His lips whispered things she couldn't hear.

"He's alive," Nessie said quietly, sitting across from her. "But his mind... is somewhere else."

"What did she do to him?"

"She tried to hollow him out. The same way she did to Selianne. The same way she did the siren. But he fought. He fought so hard, Aidina. That's the only reason he's still breathing."

Aidina lowered her head beside his.

"I'll wait," she whispered. "As long as it takes."

Rahlin didn't speak for several days.

Not even to Aidina.

He woke on the second day screaming, but not with sound. His body arched off the bed like a drowned man pulled from ice. His mouth opened, but only black air poured from it. Nessie drove the shadows back with sigils of salt and moonlight, but the wound in his mind did not close.

Aidina stayed at his side. Slept in a chair, her hand always brushing his, hoping to catch him when he surfaced.

On the sixth day, he opened his eyes.

But they were not his.

They were the sea after a storm: churned, unfamiliar, distant.

"Aidina?" he rasped. Then, softer: "Where... am I?"

She kissed his forehead. "You're home."

But home didn't mean anything to him yet. He flinched when touched. He forgot words mid-sentence. He stared at things that weren't there, feathers in the corners of rooms, a woman's voice singing lullabies in a forgotten dialect.

Each night, he dreamt of the altar.

He saw Elandra carving a spell into his chest with a comb made of bird bone.

He couldn't move. Couldn't even blink.

"You'll call her for me," she whispered, "won't you? My precious bait."

When he screamed, she fed it to herself like nectar.

Aidina would wake to find Rahlin sitting upright in bed, hands over his face, blood dripping from his nose.

Nessie watched them from the doorway. "She's left parts of herself in him. That magic... it wasn't made to wound. It was made to *replace.*"

Aidina's voice cracked. "Can you fix him?"

"I can fight the magic. But *he* has to reclaim what's his. Piece by piece."

Meanwhile, the Citadel spiraled.

The letter from the High Clan arrived in the claws of a spectral hawk. It bore the seal of Lady Virelle, one of the few leaders Visandra had tried to sway.

The message was short.

She preaches rot beneath silk. Her mentor hides in her marrow. I fear the Citadel is the target, not the cause. Prepare your people. Protect your home.

The council broke into an open argument.

"She's turning nations against us!"

"Then we strike first and force them to see the truth."

"That's suicide! We're cursed, bleeding, half-mad. If we attack now, we'll become exactly what she says we are."

Aidina sat in the council chamber, Rahlin's blood still dried on her sleeves. She felt the weight of it all bearing down, war, secrets, loss, and the worst of it:

No one trusted each other anymore.

They didn't even trust themselves.

Nessie tried to keep order, but even her voice was frayed.

"I *saw* Elandra. Fought her," she said. "She's real. She's ancient. Visandra isn't just possessed. She's *linked* to something older than the Citadel itself. She's the herald. Elandra is the storm."

Still, doubt crept in. The Black Swan Maiden was a myth to many. Even with Rahlin's condition, some council members claimed it was "mermaid illness," a weakness of the Selkie blood.

"She *nearly* killed me. Mermaid illness be damned." Madrelle responded, backing up Nessie's claim.

The council looked at each other. Their concern was more than that; it was fear. But they knew they needed to stick together, as they had for all this time. Or they would all be destroyed, one clan at a time.

Later that night, Aidina sat beside Rahlin again. He was awake but not entirely there.

"Do you remember me?" she asked.

His lips parted. He blinked hard.

"You...," he began, then stopped. "You used to... hum. Near the kelp fields. You thought no one heard."

She froze. "Yes. You always teased me about that."

"I didn't tease," he said, voice shaking. "I memorized it. In case... I had ever forgotten your face."

Aidina couldn't stop the tears.

"You came back," she whispered.

"I'm trying," he said. "She's still in there, Aidina. Somewhere. But so are you."

She held him as he trembled, both of them half-broken, both of them still fighting.

Elsewhere, beneath a canopy of dead leaves, Visandra, her darker half radiant with decay, stood before a circle of listening generals, weaving lies from truth, and truth from vengeance.

And in the dark behind her, Elandra smiled.

CHAPTER 13

The Blood Moon Daughter

The war hadn't come yet, but the wind howled like it had already begun.

The Citadel groaned under its own weight. Walls whispered. Water stirred. Citizens avoided each other's eyes. Mistrust hung like fog. The outer towers bristled with scouts, but the true enemy was already inside the castle.

Aidina hadn't slept. Not since Rahlin had first opened his eyes.

Nessie's spells had healed his body, the torn skin, the welts, the seared flesh. But his mind... his mind wandered a labyrinth made of pain and whispers. His eyes would open sometimes, focus on her face, then dart away, as if she were a hallucination he feared too much to trust.

Each time he spoke, each flicker of his soul through the shattered mirror of his body, she clung to it. But the more he remembered their stolen swims in the grotto, the time she wept into his fur cloak after a failed coronation speech, or the more his face twisted, his voice cracked. And the black magic came crawling back like a parasite reawakening inside his blood.

She begged him to fight it.

But some nights, he didn't even recognize her name.

Sometimes he spoke in riddles. Sometimes in a voice that wasn't his own.

Sometimes, he reached for her hand and then violently recoiled.

She clung to those moments. The real Rahlin was still in there. She knew it.

In the west tower, Nessie tore into the library like a woman possessed.

The books here were old enough to remember the first wars, the founding of the Citadel, and even the Vampire King's bloodline. Her fingers bled from turning pages etched in cursed ink, but she didn't care. Something was *wrong* with the air. With Rahlin. With the Citadel itself.

And then she found the book.

Bound in red leather. Laced in gold feathers. A swan's feather tucked inside the front page, charred at the tip.

Inside were the three contradicting prophecies. Written in blood that shimmered faintly under her breath.

I. Every line shall be bound by blood,
And no daughter shall be born while this prophecy lives.
For if she is, a flood of misfortune shall come,
Sweeping the land in darkness.

II. A single daughter shall emerge during a blood moon,
Born of two species.
Her heart is the beating life force of her home,
And her existence will cause the very foundations to tremble.
Dark forces will rise,

Hungry to snatch her and snuff out her light,
Believing her existence to be a curse.

III. The daughter born and killed
Will only grow in power with each revival.
She will have her lover there,
To help destroy and remake her.

Nessie stumbled back from the pages, heart pounding.

Selianne was *adopted*, and the prophecy held for her. But Aidina—Aidina was born of the King and Queen, a vampire and mermaid, the blood moon child.

And worse, the third prophecy spoke of *revival,* which meant that since Aidina had already died once, she would likely die *again.*

Her breath caught in her throat. Rahlin. If Aidina was the key, if she was the cursed miracle, then Rahlin, her bonded protector, her love, was the one meant to remake her.

By *destroying* her.

Aidina wandered the halls like a ghost, drawn toward the outer courtyard by a pull she couldn't name.

She just wanted to see the stars.

Wanted a moment where the walls weren't whispering, where Rahlin wasn't screaming in his sleep or forgetting her name. She passed an empty window and paused. A glimmer caught her eye. A figure stood beneath the trees.

Rahlin.

He was standing tall, wrapped in his usual cloak. Pale from exhaustion, but steady.

He looked up at her and smiled softly.

She gasped and rushed to him.

"You're awake. You're really awake this time?"

"I think I am," he said. "I remember... a lot."

They walked toward the water's edge, where moss and moonlight shimmered.

"I was starting to believe I'd lost you forever," she said, her voice cracking.

"I think I found myself... because of you," he replied. "Your voice brought me back."

They sat together, their reflections broken on the surface of the lake. Aidina laughed. It was a light, beautiful sound that hadn't escaped her in days.

"Remember when we used to hide in the eastern marshes?" she asked. "You used to swear that the reeds whispered your name."

"They did," he said. "They warned me. That I'd love you too much."

Nessie ran full speed inside the castle toward the council chamber, clutching the prophecy book tightly. Her breath came in ragged bursts. She had to warn them. Aidina was in danger. Everything was coming true.

She skidded to a stop at Rahlin's chamber.

Empty.

Aidina's bed was untouched.

Cold fear gripped her chest.

"No..." she whispered. "No, no, no."

She ran for the outer gates.

As the two of them walked hand in hand back to the castle, she turned to him and took his hand. Her eyes glistened. "I don't care what's happened. I don't care if you're still healing. I love you, Rahlin. I always have."

His face didn't move.

His hand, still warm in hers, tensed.

He leaned close. "And I've always protected you."

Then his other hand moved.

Aidina paused. Her body tensed. She became familiar with this feeling once more.

The blade slid into her stomach.

It was at that moment, in the War Room, that the Vampire King felt something was wrong as the Citadel started to shake. He ran into the hall and saw Nessie as she ran for the outer gates.

The sound was muffled on the castle's steps, like something underwater. Aidina's breath left her body in a strangled gasp. The world tipped.

Rahlin's face looked down at her, blank eyes glowing a haunting blue.

Not Rahlin.

Not anymore.

"She... she still has you..." she whispered, falling to her knees.

He said nothing.

He stepped closer, brushed the hair off her cheek, kissed her lips, and gently pushed her away.

She tumbled back off the stone steps, into the black marsh water.

The water rippled.

Then turned red.

The blood moon climbed above the Citadel, casting an eerie glow on the darkened land.

The wind howled through the trees like a dirge.

And the prophecy lived.

And screams echoed through the Citadel,

"Aidina!"

Coming Soon!

Coming Soon!
I hope you enjoyed the story!
Book 2: Blood Tide comes out just in time for Spooky Season!
Use the QR code below and take a look through the Shadow Library!
From signed book copies to character pages to podcasts, it's all there for you.
Enjoy and be horrified!

Scan me!